AND I PASSED M[
WITHOUT EVEN APPE

By

Naiyah Prakash

Published by DIGITAL SPINES.
Originally published by 16Leaves.

Printed and bound in India.

ADVANCE PRAISE FOR THE BOOK

And I Passed My Boards without Even Appearing for It is an excellent and well-written book by a young, dynamic and intelligent youth named Naiyah Prakash.

The concept of this book is well-thought and each chapter beautifully describes the psychological pressures and upheavals one might have gone through during the pandemic. The book provides an excellent insight into the psyche of young minds and suggests some significant opportunities to grow and glow in the line ahead. It's a must read for each child, parent and teacher. I would strongly recommend it to everyone.

Gagandeep Kaur
Presidential Gold Medalist, Double Gold Medalist
Child & Clinical Psychologist
M Phil (IHBAS)
RIC Regn. No – A10590

"Congratulations Naiyah for your achievement and I wish you great success!!"

Prakash Jha
Producer, Actor, Director & Screenwriter

"This 'fauji' kid has beautifully portrayed the bittersweet realities of the new normal through her richly crafted set of chapters and mature control over the language beyond her age."

Raghu Raman
Strategic Coach, Founder, CEO NATGRID, and Author

Advance Praise for the Book continued...

"It is truly wonderful to see how a young person has reacted to a challenging circumstance with great deal of positivity and initiative!"

Bhaskar Ramamurthi
Director, IIT Madras

"A great insight into the mind of a teenager and the challenges during a pandemic; a must read, especially for the parents of youngsters."

Bethan Sayed
Member of Welsh Parliament, 2005-21

"Inspiring writing, very eloquent style; a highly recommended read, especially in these challenging times."

Rahil Abbas
Film Producer and Chair of
Indian Commerce Chamber, Wales

Letter of Appreciation

नितिन गडकरी
NITIN GADKARI

मंत्री
सड़क परिवहन एवं राजमार्ग
भारत सरकार
Minister
Road Transport and Highways
Government of India

I am very much impressed to know that Ms. Naiyah Prakash, a student of class X, has taken the courage to put down her memories in the form of a book named – *And I Passed My Boards Without Even Appearing for It* – depicting her painful experiences and encounters as she perceives life through the thick and thin of pandemic.

The emotional and candid revelations of a young mind and the possible expectations from the society around her, in the midst of fear, panic and anxiety on account of lockdowns and social restrictions, have been beautifully portrayed in the book. I take this opportunity to call upon the young generation to keep creating such opportunities and headways even during these adverse times. It is my firm belief that our society needs new perspectives towards writing by embracing new ideas and content.

I convey my best wishes to Ms. Naiyah Prakash for a bright future and good luck in all her future endeavours.

Date: August 19, 2021
Place: New Delhi

(Nitin Gadkari)

Dr. M. Manickasamy
M.A., M. Sc., M. Ed., M. Phil, MBA, PGDG & C, DGT, PhD

केन्द्रीय विद्यालय संगठन

PRINCIPAL
Kendriya Vidyalaya, IIT Campus, Chennai

<u>Message</u>

Naiyah Prakash takes you through an inner journey of a student during the pandemic 2020, and at the same time allows one to reflect on the major changes in our schools as well! Unexpected and unprecedented situation which made the students undergo various changes affecting their physical, emotional, mental well-being have all been reflected in Naiyah's writings.

Every chapter is not just a lesson learnt for life but also a documentation on the historical transition of schooling from the physical to the virtual mode. Each and every student and their parents should read this book.

This is where you could get a peek into what it felt like being on the other side of the 'window' and look for honest feedback and perspectives, as schools move forward, aligned with the new age policy of education. It is a mental reflection of each and every student in the present situation.

Get on board with Naiyah Prakash! This is the beginning!

I wish her success in life.

Dr M Manickasamy

In loving memory of
my Nana Ji, Late Mr. Birendra Kishore Prasad
and my Mami, Late Mrs. Punam Sharad
who were very close to my heart
and whose love and support can never be equalled.
You left for your heavenly abode during these trying times
but you will continue to inspire me forever.
I promise both of you that I will make you proud.

ACKNOWLEDGEMENTS

I agree that the book finds my name on the cover, but I must confess candidly that without the encouraging words and efforts of my parents this feat of having written a book at my age could not have been possible.

My usual writing flair got a push when my mother, Dibya Prakash asked me to compile all my sincere thoughts of the pandemic time which I used to jot down on loose sheets or the last pages of the practice notebook.

The idea of getting the tag of a writer at this age was singularly so encouraging that I utilised the period of exams being cancelled to its optimum and have been able to produce something which I would surely cherish.

I would also thank my father, Ramesh Prakash, who applauded every piece of my writing and kept me pampering to propel towards the goal I had set for myself. The acknowledgement spree will not end till I make a mention of all my dear family members, friends, teachers, well-wishers and the omnipotent God to have provided me the time, space and a reason to feel happy about.

CONTENTS

PREFACE

I moved to class 10 last year. This was the year of 'possibilities' for me. It was my year, full of opportunities for a higher secondary student, full of potentials to prove myself, new things to try, get selected and represent the city or even the state in Badminton, make more friends, learn one more dialect being in Chennai and so on. I used to be so excited, pumped up and could not even wait to make my mark.

But life had something else in score for me; in fact, for all of us. This novel Coronavirus overwhelmed the world with creeping uncertainties afloat. New words like quarantine, lockdown, distancing, etc. became the order of the day. Schools became an option, Zooming a new phenomenon, Google classrooms a new norm, Badminton courts the COVID care centres and positive became the most negative word of 2020.

Initially, I took it like another flu which I envisaged would disappear soon, but with every passing day the virus found more grooves and more people, and more or less everyone on this planet felt the scare of this cruel virus.

We just kept memories of what we did, and how we shielded, kept ourselves distanced, clapped for warriors and carers, volunteered to help and stood together while maintaining distance. It was only then that I thought of penning down my encounters and experiences of the vivid COVID times; capturing the highs, lows, humour, school dreams, digital new world and many antecedents of more such bustling, lively, sometimes good and many a time of bad memories which this pandemic forced us to remember for posterity.

We missed the good old days, referred to as normal times and got used to the 'new normal'. We missed hugs, holding hands with our pals, school bus, preparation for the morning assembly amidst the routine chaos, loud laughter in substitution periods, field games, swimming periods, evening riding classes and even enjoying with parents while going to the theatres. I missed even those activities I thought I did not like.

In the year of our matriculate exams, the uncertainties kept hovering against opportunities. We toiled hard and lived everyday with the hope of going to school, living the normal life, but to our dismay, we could not even appear for the exams, the famous 'boards'. And one day, I was declared to have passed my boards without even appearing for it.

The year was really painful, leaving us on tenterhooks. The future is still unknown but we have held each other despite being at a distance for safety, survival and a better day – tomorrow.

An unexpected year it was, I passed my board examination with flying colours though. But surely I never wanted it to happen the way it was conducted, planned or thrown at us. That year where we all were tested and at different levels of exams, for some it was boards as students, livelihood as bread earners, and life at stake for the patients and so on.

And as I write this, I continue to be grateful to God for sheltering us and keeping us unscathed from the grip of this deadly virus.

Though I had geared up myself to turn last year into a timeline of attaining everything I wanted, instead it turned out to be the year in which I learned to appreciate 'everything' I have: my dear parents, family, friends and teachers.

Chapter 1

LOCKDOWN: CONFINED FOR WELLBEING

I could faintly make out the correct answer to the question and perhaps that is the advantage of having multiple choice questions listed during the exam as you can exercise your guessing ability on the basis of partial knowledge of the topic, to some extent. I was in the midst of my final exam schedule, writing my General Knowledge paper when I was confronted with a question about the Coronavirus. Having read about it in an article before, I somehow ticked the right answer. But much to my disbelief, when the answers were discussed in the class, most of my classmates got the answer wrong. Perhaps, not many had given much significance to that viral outbreak in China, which was a less known affair then. It was taken as some petty new viral flu confined to mainland China and later to some western countries. But who knew that this much-passed-over news bite was going to be the major driving factor for the abrupt change in everybody's life in times ahead.

February 2020; yes more precisely the 26th day – I vividly cherish those last few hours being at school, when I had finished my term-ending final exams of standard nine. I was relieved to finish off the tiring exam sessions and the idea of some relaxation was more the merrier to soothe my soul from the extremely hard toil of the exhausting exam schedule. I remember this last day of the exam, wherein my friends and I were making elaborate plans of how we would spend the entire vacation enjoying and not devoting any of our precious time to studies! On being asked about her plans for the forthcoming vacation, a friend of mine exclaimed, "I would just rest for the entire first week, not even looking at my course books. I am so happy to finally have a break from school for some time!" Had she been told that she would not be able to go to school for a year, she would have regretted saying that. But none of us could guess what had been awaiting us! A Pandemic!

On 24 March 2020, I was sitting comfortably on the sofa, watching television. Just then my father asked me to change the channel; probably he wanted to watch the news. Unwillingly, I handed him the remote. As he surfed the news channels, we were surprised to find the same address being flashed everywhere. We stopped at one, listening to our Honourable Prime Minister who announced, "My countrymen, we are in the midst of this viral epidemic because of the deadly coronavirus ...." Before we could react, a nationwide 'lockdown' for 21 days, limiting movement of the entire population, was imposed as a preventive measure to contain the viral spread. People were forced to put off their work and subsequently advised to be confined at home. Like me, not many could understand and expect what this viral infection had in store for the entire gentry. Actually, it was just the tip of the iceberg! The present seemed something akin to an unfathomable truth to us, then.

We had never heard of the word 'lockdown', which had suddenly been imposed to contain the spread. Out of curiosity, I used the same old trusted 'Google' to find what exactly it was. The definition clearly implied that it was a restriction policy for people to stay where they were, usually due to some specific risk. And this time the pretext was outspread of a novel virus. It seemed so much fatal to the authorities that they literally 'closed' the nation, not giving priority to the consequent economic setback likely to be triggered. It was only when we got to know about the casualties and fatalities continuously being displayed on the news bulletin that we understood the reason behind the government's abrupt move.

I remember to be sitting in my balcony, looking expectantly onto the road leading the way out of my dwelling. It was the same route that I undertook dozens of times in a day to move in and out. But now, it seemed empty, with nearly no footfall. It had been a week since the confinement began, cutting us off from the external world. One of the few things that comforted us was the newspaper that was delivered to us, ensuring daily updates. Our old hawker-*bhaiya* used to throw it at our newspaper stand perfectly with that same precision,

letting it land in the stack. The only change I observed was a sizable mask, now complementing his exhausted visage. The newspapers used to be flooded with disheartening figures of leaping COVID cases and heart-wrenching anecdotes of migrant workers, heading home on the double, facing innumerable difficulties on the way.

As most of the economic activities had been put to a standstill, many daily wage earners started rushing back to their native villages. Having no source to earn, left them pauperised to an extent, they could not survive in the prevalent situation. The migrants or the guest workers as everybody called them for the services they provided to the people, away from their own place, 'risked their lives to live', with at least the hope of breathing their last at home.

The initial curfew gave many of us the idea of what was going to happen in the subsequent days. We realised that we would not be able to continue with our routine life while being out of it and the testing period of our lives had shown up. It was a complete 'no movement' situation. The scary tales of curfew during freedom movements or after any riot or arson which we had learned about in text books came alive vividly to our mind.

After the lockdown was imposed, I remember one of my friends from another school talking about the cancellation of his last papers due to surging COVID cases and another one mischievously conveying about the possibility of being promoted to the next class, without even appearing for all the exams. One of them teasingly remarked, "How unfortunate you people have been, all of you had to write all your exams and I had a good narrow escape!" while the other replied, "Good for you; the government policy has helped you move up to the next class or you would have been kept back!" which was followed by a boisterous laugh in unison. Apart from these bittersweet truths, there were numerous speculations in the air, keeping us sceptical about the reality. So the rumours in the air, not only about exams but also about various other aspects, had begun to do rounds.

And what followed was unexpectedly expected! Our school which had been shut took an online form. Even other works related to living resumed digitally. As much as I say, it would not be sufficient but the government's vision of 'Digital India' had taken a stage for soaring high. The golden opportunities could be visualised in days of adversity created by the pandemic. Since we could no longer step out of our houses, the social interactions had become virtual through various online platforms like Zoom, Google Meet and so on, which were making their presence felt globally. And we humans had become helplessly dependent on these platforms to communicate while socially distancing ourselves. Initially, we tried our best to live normally in the 'new normal' world which had become devoid of human touch, mostly connected through the sole alternative, that is, via the internet. But gradually we were getting fed up with the anguish that we were gripped into.

This was also the time when we quickly took to the unwanted soap operas and daily TV shows, which used to be broadcasted instead of the regular ones. During those days, people had willingly attuned to the recast of Ramanand Sagar's *Ramayana*, B R Chopra's *Mahabharata* and other epics, despite them having no high definition quality that people nowadays seek!

I remember it had only been a year since my father's posting when I was getting accustomed to my new school with my new friends at Chennai, who were giving me lessons to communicate in the local and 'new' adopted language, that the lockdown was imposed. Before coming to this place, I had never understood the true essence and usage of the local language. As much to my dismay, only occasionally had my classmates been conversing in English, mostly talking to each other in Tamil only. To be able to understand everything, I made it a point to learn the language soon. Accordingly, I kicked off my learning program, taking interest in their opaque conversations initially and later trying to get the hang of it. Apart from the language, the accent also had to be learnt, to sound more colloquial. As a practice, I started greeting my friends, saying, "*Vanakkam macha!*" To which, they used to heartily respond, "Yaar, did you wish your previous school friends with *namaste* or simply *hi?*"

But had I known that not only this but even going to school was going to be on hold, I wouldn't have put in so much of my energy and mind into it! All my efforts in vain! And as it is we move to a new place every two years, being from an army background; I would not be able to make use of it, further. Other things, I can recollect of being stranded midway were swimming classes, riding sessions and badminton coaching, which I used to love to be engaging in. Once we were done with our exams, my gang of pals had made a plan of having an outing. We were to go for a movie and Café Coffee Day, all by ourselves to enjoy the holidays. But that too had to be called off, owing to the curbs.

Although our lives had changed considerably, I was in a comparatively better condition than most of my civilian friends as then I could at least venture out inside the walled premises of the army cantonment, which was out of bounds for others, creating a sort of bio bubble, which we later derived. Whilst most of the professions had been put to a standstill, my father was still going to the office as usual and we, children could be out for cycling on the deserted periphery road, though unlike the normal days, taking utmost precautions like wearing masks and keeping a safe distance. I used to remind myself of these small free movements, especially at times when I used to feel despondent, having no control of the circumstances thrown at us.

To perceive everything from an optimist's point of view, whatever happens, it is for good and therefore fretting over something we cannot control is useless. Adjusting to it and putting the best of our efforts are the only ways we can adopt at times like this!!

Chapter 2

Digital Classrooms: New Form but Old Stunts

I was gazing at my computer screen, trying to unearth the motivation to turn it on. Each time I tried, my fingers recoiled before making a contact with the power button, lying at rest. It was time for my online classes to begin. It was going to be yet another day of mine, spending hours staring at the tiny boxes displaying our tired faces, already disturbed with the burden of previous assignments. And now we had to attempt holding onto the concepts that would be taught to us. The same readiness of pressing the leave button, before the humdrum lecture began, would be presented in my mind yet again. But I would have to sit there, in my exclusive study room, in my cold wooden desk, ready to learn online even then.

I remember that we had a lesson in our English Supplementary reader last year, titled 'The Fun They Had' by Isaac Asimov. It was a short story in the science fiction genre which was set in the future. It took us into a world where robots and computers were used instead of human teachers and textbooks. Though we have not forged ahead up to the extent which the author, Isaac Asimov had predicted, the pandemic has certainly pushed us to a corner which we would have taken at least a decade or two to advance to in the normal routine pace of development. As said earlier, our school curriculum had also become online, the classes and assignments were given to us on classroom apps and we were to make sure that we handed in the assigned work on time as the teachers could no longer supervise us in person! The unconventional classes commenced soon after a month, once we were promoted to class 10. Owing to the prevalent situation, our school had made it mandatory to conduct the subject classes only and no co-curricular sessions as it was not pragmatic to conduct such classes online. All this marked the beginning of the 'end of our physical bonhomie' in the classroom. And since it was primarily based on distanced learning, it did not require us to commute through our bus to make it to the school, preventing us from enjoying the daily school bus ride. The bus ride meant endless gossiping, cracking of jokes and frolicking games that could be played while the bus was still in motion. It also meant unending discussions about the burning topics at school, and about teachers or other fads.

Going to the school physically has no substitute. But the online-turned school was not as bad as presumed by many of us initially. Despite lacking direct social connect and interaction, this had proved to be the sole medium of learning. I could recollect the good old school days when we used to spend most of our time rejoicing and playing in the substitution periods! Those were in fact the most awaited periods! But these online classes had made it more or less impossible to have a day off for us, which usually happened when any of our subject teachers were absent. However since teachers too taught from the comfort of their homes, the substitution periods could not be expected very often!

The Online mode classes through 'Digital Classroom' used to be organised with adequate breaks in between to ensure that not much strain was given to the eyes of the studious children, but despite that nearly half of my class wears spectacles now, and that includes me!

The most interesting part of these classes was that the students had devised new methods here too, to stay ahead of the teachers with their ever humorous and plausible excuses. One of the most practiced methods was not turning on the video mode during the online classes and responding to what is being asked. I reminisce the first fortnight when our teacher asked a naughty boy of our class to convey the answer, he texted in the chat box "Sorry ma'am, I can't answer because I am suffering from mike problem", as if he had seasonal flu! Not only this, the justification for almost everything was connectivity issue and its severity varied from the ability of each to make it as realistic as feasible by getting disconnected during the call, time and again. Needless to say, some had real genuine problems too. Also, this way even many of the active participants of our class became passive, displaying this on occasions when the teacher asked questions like "Is anyone there in the class?" or "Am I audible?" just after speaking at

length and not getting any reply at all. However, at times the class used to get interrupted by unnecessary background noises and voices of people in the vicinity divulging information about the student's location. And once, one of our innocent classmates carelessly forgot to turn off his audio, revealing that he had kept his phone somewhere near the cricket pitch where he was batting!

While we had just begun with the online classes, we were not used to the signs or symbols for various modes, we had later come to memorise them by heart! In one of such initial online classes, I was mistaken to have texted the wrong person, finding that the chosen icon was not our friend Kirti but our Maths teacher Kavya ma'am! I didn't blame myself as both of their turned-off video icons were represented by the letter 'K'! That time none of us had a profile picture displaying our styled selves, only later did our classmates find the online class platform as yet another medium to post their cool photos! Initially, this unfamiliarity with the platform often exposed personal text messages sent to some friend to the whole class, which derived humour out of our undone conversation. Sometimes that cost us heavily, getting severe admonishment from the teacher for talking during the class.

On more than one occasion, our class had been given the rare experiences of accommodating unbidden imposters! And the spammers were also present to enthrall us and annoy our teachers with their invalid yet humorous texts! There were days when a period or two used to be spent on inspection of the spammers followed by a detailed investigation on the basis of suspicion of a few trusted adherents of the teacher! It was indeed interesting to figure out how the age-old mike problem used to vanish suddenly when it came to holding someone responsible for the mischief! Our 'Google' classroom used to become a courtroom with a person becoming the public prosecutor, presenting arguments against the momentarily made defence lawyer, trying to prove someone's innocence. But after all, the final decision was made by our class teacher, the judge who had the authority to give rigorous punishment of attending extra classes at odd hours to the convicted!! And thus justice would be ensured, completing a fair trial!!

Initially, it was disheartening for the teachers to talk in a hushed class with not a single soul acknowledging them, but with some experience as they got going, they began to understand and respond to all the mischief with their innovative but ephemeral ideas. While it was practically unbelievable for us to keep quiet in our routine classes, with the online classes coming in order, our innate penchant of incessant talking almost vanished!

Although we had been compelled to shift to this mode of learning, longing for a return to the normal one persisted. Serving as a class, the 'online classroom' could not take the position held by our bustling morning assemblies which used to charge us with rejuvenating morale for the rest of the day and the keenly awaited sports period that always contained the excitement and liberty for us to whoop it up.

All this had been a new experience for everyone and gradually we had adopted it or rather got adapted to it. But the real school with chalk and duster learning was way better than the one we were now getting used to.

Chapter 3

MISSING THE GANG: FRIENDS FOREVER

With a sense of pride, I can boast to have seen a minimum of eight schools in my experience of 12 years of schooling. All through these years, I have met many new faces, distributed along the lengths and breadths of the country. Those once-unfamiliar folks became my friends forever; I still connect with them and fondly relive those episodes of camaraderie spent together. Being an army brat, I have seen a large proportion of the country because of my father's regular biannual postings and I am fortunate to have made friends from many regions, of many dialects and covering all types of schools, that is, from private ones to government schools, Army Public Schools, KVs, co-ed and what not. Diversity of the novel locations that came by ensured new friends, with new aspirations and hopes to sail through, experiencing all joys and glooms together. For a mere instance, when my cousins or relatives narrate about the same old friends or school each vacation, I start off with yet another comic tale of my newly made friends. It is fun indeed to have so many friends since childhood but the undeniable truth of moving to a new place each time also compels army brats like me to secretly detest the fact that we have no 'childhood' friends who have been with us, all the years since nursery! However, we know that our pals are like stars, they may not be present all the while, but are always there for us!

Craving for friends had surely been experienced during this pandemic phase, wherein we were set afar, forbidding us to be with our schoolmates, playmates and those trustworthy faces, with whom we used to spend so much of our time. And then, we were so caught up in our studies and board preparations that we hardly got any time to spend with them, even through FaceTime. Despite the willingness to stay in touch constantly, we had been compellingly distanced due to these unfortunate circumstances. I can dearly recollect the days when we used to enjoy our entire time at school, weaving jolly tales and enjoying our precious time to the fullest. Besides studies obviously, meeting friends used to be one of the principal reasons for going to school. Even when we used to feel like taking a day off, the longing to engage in mischief or gossip with our dear buddies used to make us change our minds! A mere thought of a close friend could make us forget about any distress! But hunched over with the burden of high school studies and pandemic anxiety, we had been missing our friends even more. And we were not able to be with each other when we needed that sort of escort the most; an ironical situation indeed!

I reminisce the day when my friends and I had planned to do a video call but that had to be called off due to the sudden announcement and conduct of an extra class! We were thoroughly dejected as the date and time for the much-awaited call had been finalised after due deliberation, thinking of a suitable holiday when there were not many assignments to worry about! But that too had to be put out, courtesy of our class teacher, who despised the talkative temperament of our class. And even in the lockdown, our suspicion in this regard was proved to be correct, as she made sure that the fixture of the extra classes coincided with our conference call, four out of five times!

I fondly recollect one of those 'few' days when we finally availed the opportunity to have a conference video call not just for the sake of a chat but for making plans for one of our gang member's forthcoming birthday celebrations on a virtual medium. We started with, "You have to arrange for a present. Confirm before ordering it." Along with, "Make sure that you don't forget to make the collage, I'll remind you for being on the safer side!" We tried our best not to fail in making her day special as it was probably the first time she would literally not have any grand celebrations on the day. As the day dawned, we tried our best to engage her in all the celebrations we had planned. Our efforts had paid, making us immensely gratified to find a beam of satisfaction on her face. That day, we even teased her for having a lockdown birthday but who knew that the pandemic would extend further, engulfing our birthdays too!

Remembering about friends, the first thing that comes to my mind is having a good time and utilising each moment to enjoy. It used to be a moment of respite, listening to those meaningless jokes during class when each word used to be said cautiously, minding the teacher's attention, marked by our pals' incessant tendency to reach out for the book at the right time! And the real fun used to charge in when the teacher used to suspect our fake innocence and clinging onto the textbook for a long time, provoking us to get caught! Apart from this, it was always the in-class secretive but collective lunch that used to quench our hunger!

We had a close-knit understanding of each other's secrets, nick names, code words and mischievous plans, which could

sometimes land us in soup, and we would be appropriately fixed and reprimanded by our dear parents! Even during the pandemic, the phone calls continued, though infrequent, till we were done with nearly all the details of our everyday life. And now, the day-long fixture of talking was replaced by a limited number of calls, few FaceTime and video conferencing meets, brief texts and shrill audio messages. Even the immemorial tradition of jokes was substituted by those forwarded memes.

And as fights are common in all friendships, we were all well acquainted with each other's periodical angry outbursts, death stares and subsequent pleading looks and set of apologetic words. Their not-so-frequent cheeky but prudent comments were ample to ponder over! Even if they appeared to be rude, they prepared us for a harsh reality lying ahead. Taking a trip down my memory lane, I could recollect the times when my pals used to share our punishments by participating in the mischief! I can recall some of them saying, though only for missing out the class themselves, "Ma'am, even I didn't bring the notebook, I am equally liable of receiving the punishment, aren't I?" and at times turning the new leaf suddenly, complaining, "Ma'am, so and so were involved in the fight, I have witnessed it completely," making us realise our faults and forcing us to hone ourselves. Those days in the 'real' school will remain etched in our memory forever!!

Friends are like rainbows in our cloud, cultivating colours of hope, happiness and positive vibes in our lives. Not only do they motivate us, but also aid us in striving for the accomplishment of our goals. Friendship is truly an unconditional bond of love!!

Hearing tales of how people put their lives at stake to help their friends come out of this pandemic adversity sensitises and motivates us. The 'many' inspiring incidents of people who showed their bonds even from long distances set up a flame of hope that reminds us that we would soon be with our pals, post fighting the contagion with full might. We see that altruism and the 'bonding' exist even on being set afar by the present circumstances. It gives us hope and belief that being distanced from our friends, we were linked through a nexus of hearts and bond from within!!!

Chapter 4

QUARANTINE: WHEN PROTECTION BECOMES REPRESSION

The real fear and test of my family and others in the army cantonment commenced when one of the security personnel tested positive for the novel coronavirus, as we had been following all requisite protocols and taken necessary precautions not to breach the bio bubble. The courtesy meetings with one another, maintaining due social distancing and prescribed protocols to an extent, were on. But the specific case forced us to confine ourselves at our respective complexes completely. It was made so strict because one person testing positive could invite a series of high and low risk contacts to be monitored and later quarantined. Correlating the concepts that took refuge in our 'matriculate' brains, I realised that the spread of the coronavirus was something akin to geometric progression and not the arithmetic one, thus creating an environment of concern. We were well aware of the fact that soon the cases in our vicinity would grow at a pacing rate, making ourselves fall in line without any doubt.

This made us captives at our own abode, in a total locked up state. Sitting in our lawn, we could not hear the usual honking, voices of people babbling or the hysterical laughter of children in the vicinity. It was as if the stern measures were mandated not to contain the viral infection but to disturb our normal lives. All I could notice through my see-through green fence was a pack of stray dogs, engaged in their jovial free-for-alls on the muffled street, void of any passerby.

This period of quarantine was considered disgusting as initially I found it humanly impossible to stay at one place until everything was back to normal, which took some real hard days to get accustomed to living safely. The thought of spending the 'entire' day at one place was unconditionally scary. I was beginning to put myself in *Anne Frank's* shoes as even she was pushed to her limits whilst in hiding. Though we, in the present scenario, were in a far better place as we didn't have to hide against persecutions, we were, to some degree, in a similar state. But in Anne's situation the catastrophe wasn't caused by a mere virus but due to the Nazi perpetrators being driven by an unreasonable hatred for the Jews. It was especially when I used to find myself gazing at the walls of my well-decorated room that appeared to remind me that I had to spend my entire time staying indoors!

A new word entered into the vocabulary of our daily life: 'Quarantine'. As per the dictionary, the word meant a period of isolation in which people or animals that have arrived from elsewhere or been exposed to infectious or contagious diseases are placed. But we used that dreaded term reluctantly to convey our prevalent state of being. Although even before, much of our movement was restricted, the prevailing situation had been made worse, making us believe that we were in lockup and not in lockdown!

In the first few days of our encounter with our totally changed life, there used to be a frown on my 'always smiling' visage, indicating my helplessness. But my father comforted me by telling me about the army personnel who are posted at the line of control or the glacier in an ice-chilling and back-breaking cold environment with no luxuries at all. Referring to their condition, he told me that they stay in the same bunker, to prevent being shelled by the enemy, for months in conditions we can't think of, even in our wildest dreams! And the best part is that they don't crib like us. That made me realise that we are in a way better state, although it had never been so bad like this, and it would soon be over if we face it with courage and hope!

So despite the curbs and the mental fatigue caused by the stern measures to tackle the spread, we didn't sulk. My parents and I tried different things to make ourselves busy and occupied so that the dire straits passed without being felt.

Right from the beginning, we made a firm resolution that we would start our day by exercising in the morning, which would be followed by everyone's involvement in preparing the meals for the whole day. I was the one who got to be exposed to cooking as I was rather a novice, barely having any culinary

experience until then! In the first instance, I was just made to potter about under my parents' instructions for fetching veggies from the refrigerator, spices from the shelf and mere cutleries from the racks. Later, when it was almost a week of mine, doing nothing really significant, I took a step forward towards my journey in the making of a chef! And since then I have been contributing my little skills whenever required. So in a way, this quarantine and lockdown life forced me to hone one of the most requisite life skills, which is too important for sustenance.

My parents and I binge-watched some web series and played cards and board games. All this proved essential in dodging the bullet, in terms of getting relieved of all sort of stress. We utilised this time in engaging ourselves in our hobbies, which we were not able to pursue regularly due to the hectic schedule. My father and I collectively painted two canvases and got them framed, giving our minds a sense of satisfaction and composure. I even called my old friends and relived those good old memories and fabulous days spent in bygone days at former schools. Only the first word seemed to come out hesitatingly, realising that I talked for an hour with those friends, whom I had not spoken to for a year!

This period also made us live devoid of our domestic helps, making all of us run errands in place of our maids! Thus, washing utensils and mopping the floor became some of our routine chores in quarantine. I came to realise the significance of the role played by all these people to make our lives comfortable, but who are normally taken for granted and not respected for the work they perform. With some apprehensions at first, I settled to wash the utensils after some of the meal sessions and assisted my parents in cleaning and mopping the house, making it look squeaky clean! This could only be possible when I comprehended that I should also help in such tasks since no work was inferior to the other.

Besides these routine chores, I kicked off a project that I had never accomplished on my own, which was growing organic and garden-fresh veggies in my kitchen garden. Although I had witnessed the plants grow before, I never took much interest in doing it myself. But this time, I devoted my time to sowing and watering the plants daily, ensuring that they were nurtured properly. Experiencing the joy of planting for the first instance and seeing the sapling grow into a healthy plant, I was really overwhelmed and felt like a dog with two tails! Moreover, I also prepared a 'compost pit' by putting in all the segregated bio waste in a pit in my backyard.

This phase taught me a lot, like respecting whatever we had, cultivating life skills, getting the hang of household chores, developing practical skills based on theoretical knowledge, and so on; turned out to be of immense significance. The quarantine days, though hard, strengthened everyone's family bonds and so was a case in my house. Due to everyone's work and commitments, we never got to spend so much time with each other. And much to our disbelief, we didn't even realise that the much dreaded quarantine period was thoroughly enjoyed at home!

Chapter 5

THE E-SUPPLIES: LIVING IN THE LOCKDOWN MODE

Although the inaccessibility of all the essential supplies didn't pinch us during the total lockdown days, there was indeed some stuff that particularly I was yearning for. Asking for something without which we could survive was not at all wise, especially when routine supplies and services were inadequate. So being cognisant, I suppressed my desire to have non-vegan food for nearly three months! This was undeniably a long time, for someone like me who just could not do without non-vegetarian food for even a few days! As I have always loved eating such foods, it was a very tough time for me. And giving credence to those sparking news feeds, showing how celebrities were turning vegan, was unbelievable for me! But in my case, it was by chance and not by choice, even for a few weeks!

Besides the food inaccessibility or shortage, as it is called, there were a lot of other things whose supplies, concerning children and their parents, were scarce like textbooks, scrapbooks, record notebooks and stationeries. I remember few of my friends in junior classes, asking for my previous grades' course books as they could not buy those essentially needed hardbound books for the new session as the lockdown was imposed soon after the term-ending exams of the previous standard, leaving no time for planning and buying those 'then-overlooked' things. But luckily my mother had bought all the books and other stationery items much before the beginning of the new session to ensure that we got everything in time, avoiding the crowded shops and exhausting of the items, as happened during our previous visits to the book stores. The usual scene at any store that time used to be a sight of tired parents falling in line to get their share of books from the busy shopkeepers. And luckily we did not have to worry about either of the situations like others and the entire credit goes to my mother for her fine eyes for detail and planning!

Even before the pandemic, online marketing was on its way, impressing customers and increasing its following. But as the embargos were put in order, even the customers who always used to depend upon their in-shop marketing skills were made to count on the online shopping sites, with no alternatives available. And thus the requirement of home supplies, grocery or clothing items entirely depended on the online mode. I still remember how initially when some ordered stuff arrived at our house, we used to tell the delivery person to keep it outside the door and then we let it exposed to the sun for hours as if the virus was scared of the scorching sunlight! Perhaps we had trusted an unexplained forwarded theory! The initial craziness about online delivery made us sanitise each article that came our way, using those disinfectants whose odour could make us feel giddy! Also, we strictly avoided outside *Swiggy* or *Zomato* food to be on the safer side, assuming that the viral strains were used instead of spices! Only later were we acquainted with the truth, ignoring rumoured misconceptions.

Though online shopping had always been an awesome option, later the delivery in our locality was stopped as our locality was marked as a containment zone because of the escalating number of COVID cases. We had no choice but to live with the old ones for our clothing, apparel, shoes and all. We could still manage using the same clothes, but infants or newly born babies in the vicinity born post-January 2020, who generally grew tall pretty fast in a matter of few months, had a really difficult time continuing with the same old clothes. If I can recollect correctly, an aunt in my neighborhood, used the frocks of her five-year-old daughter to stitch jumpsuits for her infant baby! Indeed necessity is the mother of invention! Talking of clothes, informals like pajamas and tees had become the fad, compelling everyone to stay in comfortable attires as there was no going out for anyone! Even for online classes, only the upper half would remain formal, leaving the bottom invisible half in cosy night suits! The idea of stylish clothes had suddenly dwindled as comfortables were reigning styled attires!

Some amusing tales account for the troublesome period for those who were deprived of their beauty products and the difference could be felt just by looking at their visages! An acquaintance of mine, with no available resources, had to step out of her house with her unusually grey hair which used to be shining black before, courtesy dyes and salon bays shut during that time! And all the beauty queens had to do with homemade *haldi* pastes rather than the regime facials!

Although now various designs of masks are available in the market, with the advent of the pandemic, only surgical masks could be found everywhere, compelling us to wear those simple sizeable masks. So I, with an artistic soul, tried fabric paints to tie-and-dye, making a designer cloth piece which was further stitched in the form of a mask by my mother. Appropriately, a fully homemade mask, with no marketed stuff other than the cloth and paints, was finally ready to use. It was fun to wear my own creation, as per my design and taste of colour!

In addition to a lot of things being out of reach, a few facilities and amenities were also not being availed like that of washer men and barbers. We were unable to reach out to our old hairdressers at salons, thereby making our homes our new salons. And likewise, my mother tried her hands at dressing my father's and my hair. It was a new yet enticing experience for us. Though there were apprehensions regarding this trimming of hair by a novice, later we agreed upon it and sat silently draped in a cloth so as not to get exposed to hair all over our body, taking ideas from our former visits to the salon! And surprisingly my mother styled my hair like a professional hairdresser as if she had ample working experience in the field!

Astoundingly, the gross expenditure at the home front was also at all-time low because of a fortuitous decline in expenses, as most of the work was undertaken at home with the help of family labour! Household resources were utilised and unnecessary outlay was forbidden due to the lockdown restrictions and health concerns!

Apparently, that was how things were, entirely out of our control. Not considering the situation we were suddenly forced into, a bane completely, we learnt a lot, especially adjusting with whatever we had and making the fullest use of all the resources available. Apart from this, we got enough time for introspection of how we can try to do most of our things ourselves, yet we shy away to discharge our sincere efforts in making our lives self-reliant, in true ways. We actually realised that 'less' was 'more' to survive.

Chapter 6

THE WHAT TO DO SYNDROME

With the COVID cases surging at an exponential pace across the globe, especially during those peak summer months, the environment around was in total mess. With lockdowns, unheard therapies and newly devised norms becoming the order of the day, it seemed that nothing could be done to get back to the same old world of ours.

Added to this misery, there were other things for me to worry about, ranging from the urgency to submit the school assignments to the news that I had just been fed with. It was delivered to me by one of my friends, who stayed in my neighbourhood. I remember the occasion well; it was when she came running to me with a downcast face, making me anxious until she stopped at my door, sighing hard to let the words come out effortlessly. And guess what, she had come to inform me that her father had got his posting orders; perhaps the time to bid her farewell had come. My face reciprocated with the same look as hers, realising that a close friend, who happened to be one of my few friends, was present with me during the lockdown distress. The friends who stayed close by were the only ones I was able to meet, for a few playful moments though. Their company was one of the few comforting aspects of the stern restrictions as meeting school friends had not been a privilege we could afford, leaving only the camaraderie of the ones staying just a stone's throw away. And now even one of them was leaving! It was disheartening to know that we would not meet each other until the next opportunity, which might not be anytime soon. But over the years, we, army kids have been accustomed to leaving friends and moving on to find new ones. It has become a part and parcel of our lives, teaching us big life lessons from these small events in our life that we encounter frequently.

And in a train of a similar chance of events, I could not even continue playing any sort of outdoor game or a sport, to engage and divert my aching soul in the monotonous evenings, with no thrill. I can remember myself doing nothing in the evenings and whiling away time just like that as one cannot even study for the entire day. Doing some physical exercise or indulging in sports is required to ensure proper maintenance of the mind and body. But where the need of the hour was to save and protect lives from falling prey to the deadly viral infection, the urge to maintain it would obviously never be that potent! Remembering my evenings before the pandemic, I could not remember a single day when I was not busy playing, running or cycling. I have always been fond of sports and could not refrain from playing for too long. Normally, by the time it's evening, I am in my sportswear, ever ready to sweat! But my evening regime had entirely been disrupted due to the inevitable pandemic.

Badminton, which has been one of my favourite sports since childhood, was also being missed– the running to and fro on the sturdy court to reach the feathered shuttle. But as the guidelines for the curbs were imposed, all sportsgrounds, courts, movie halls and stadiums had been shut to ensure that the infections do not spread further. Only emergency services had been functioning at their routine pace, other activities had been closed and thereby the badminton courts in the cantonment too were shut. The courts and sports complexes, which were once devoted solely for accommodating players, charging in with their drills, were made into COVID care centres to attend the patients battling COVID. It was reassuring to find that they were catering to the requirements of the medic staff while treating ailing patients. So there came a time when I could not play with my friends and keep up my badminton practice, it was indeed monotonous to do nothing but hope for things to improve, if not be normal.

Moreover, we, children could not even play online games the entire free time because the screen time was mostly utilised for online classes, and that was enough to cause pain in our eyes, force an uncomfortable posture and affect overall health, in some way or the other. And the time which I once solely spent on outdoor games was wasted doing nothing significant, not even these games! Talking to some of my friends, I came to know that the smart ones were using the pandemic as an excuse to keep themselves busy with the games like GTA,

PUBG, Among Us, Freefire, Minecraft, Ludo King and so on! And seeing the situation, their parents were readily agreeing to their demand, evidently wanting them to feel relieved from the 'contagious' stress of confinement and uncertainty triggered by the pandemic. Focusing on outdoor games, the ones like cricket and football had resumed at the national and international front a little later but in our case, it was still based on our ability to take a risk, not knowing if our playmates were by any chance, 'corona carriers'. And sports like swimming had become a kind of dream as even in the near future, the possibility of its commencement for amateurs like us was rather unlikely!

The stress was enough to necessitate innovative ideas and taking a trip down my memory lane, and I can remember having come up with an idea of taking a virtual tour of a distanced location as going physically could not be thought of as an option. Though stupid, it proved to be an alternative to the real tour, akin to other 'proxies' for all the activities which we once exhibited on the ground! To name a few, I paid a visit to Switzerland and Italy just by sitting in front of my TV, relying on my home theatre! The 8K resolution quality gave a sense of satisfaction to at least one of my sensory organs –my eyes – that were wide open to grasp the eternal beauty of the places, virtually.

To sum it up, there was nothing other than stress, which we could cultivate even during those unlock phases of lockdown! It may seem easy but the dynamic confinement left an undeniable mental setback on children like us. The fear of the unknown was becoming evident and known! After all, living a life like this had never been taught to us, this was something we could not cope up with! And the anxiety was getting the better of us.

Chapter 7

MY ALMA MATER:
BEING A KV-ITE

In my myriad thoughts, I came to realise that though I have portrayed my friends, teachers, classes and everyday affairs a thousand times, I couldn't elaborate upon the institution, where most of it happened. Yes, to be honest, I feel enthralled and proud to be part of the school which taught me so much; not only on the academic front but also relating the social fabric while offline or on online mode. KV IIT; Kendriya Vidyalaya, IIT Chennai to be precise, pushed me to sail through my high school experience. When my father got posted to Chennai, I was enrolled in KVIIT Chennai which is one of the most reputed schools in the country, known for its excellence in academics. It is located inside IIT Madras campus, near Guindy; a suburb in south-western part of Chennai.

There are ten to twelve KVs here in Chennai, but KV IIT campus – my alma mater – was a signature address to be attached to. Presumably, it was told that a maximum of students preferred science subjects in their 11th and 12th classes, appeared for IIT entrance exams and got selected to take disciplines undertaken by IIT, Madras for graduation. I don't know why but I carried a different conception and always ensured that I would take humanities in higher secondary as main subjects, though just to mention, I would get nearly 100% in my Mathematics and Science subjects for sure.

Kendriya Vidyalaya or popularly known as KV actually provides an essence of unity in diversity. The central government employees who travel throughout the lengths and breadths of the country every two or three years provide school facilities to their wards in these KVs. So in a nutshell, we find an amalgam of cultural, social, demographical synthesis in the school. And with this essence, we learn about different cultures, languages and living in the best-illustrated manner. Even the teachers are posted based on all India class representation, which makes the best arrangement we can think of. So while my father got posted to Chennai and once I found myself landed at KV IIT Chennai, I did not find myself concerned about the change for long; rather I, in no time, was finding myself elated, to have experienced altogether ninth change of school in my 12 years of schooling life. I could assure that whilst I was in Chennai, I would have a good time, schooling here. And I had to get accustomed to the new culture and most importantly the lingo here. Initially, I thought that I would not be able to continue with my talkative frenzy, but in no time I found myself adjusted with my new friends, to have a wonderful experience at high school.

Apart from being known for the academics, my school excelled in sports as well as co-curricular activities and I did not realise it until I got into the muddle to experience the same. It had not even been a week since my admission to the school when we were told to run 5 rounds of the 'huge' ground in the PHE period to warm ourselves up before some real game. It was a boiling summer with sultry conditions and I had not yet got acclimatised to the new climate and thus despite having the endurance and stamina, I could hardly complete it in time. Once, I reached the finishing line, I had to straightaway go to the medical intervention room to get checked as I was on the verge of getting a faint! I looked as if the whole of my energy had been squeezed out of me like a lemon, which is used to prepare lime water! And that was what I was given to rehydrate my dehydrated self! But mind it, relentless our sports teacher was and so were we, with dogged determination that I was included in the school team in a week, and was told in a pre-match lecture, "We have to be prepared for the worst; so at least give it a try, as we have always excelled." Luckily, I was part of the Girls' Basketball Team of the school.

The IIT campus, wherein our school is located, has been adorned with greenery as far as the eyes can see, with thousands of species of flora and fauna as its natural habitat. When I was going to school for the first time, I was amazed to find a herd of deer crossing the road and much to my surprise, it was a usual experience for other co-travelling students of my bus. Later I came to know that the campus was their home and they roam about freely everywhere, be it on the road or the school playground. To my surprise, I found billboards on the road saying "Animals have the right of way". Truly empathetic. The environment was serene and calm but marked by omnipresent quiet and innocent deer and even monkeys, who were always exuberant to seek attention. Quite often they used to intrude in our class and were welcomed with shrieks and stamping of feet. When they used to enter our class, it used to get converted into a real fish market with people hurrying to get out. The chaos in the class could only be settled when the monkeys, having no pleasurable sight would be ready to depart! Here, I noticed my classmates bringing a separate lunch bag along with the routine school bag, unlike prevalent elsewhere. And before I discovered that, monkeys had already made a plan to steal this belonging of theirs. One day, while my class was returning from the computer lab, we were fearfully surprised to find the empty tiffin boxes taken out of the bag and thrown on the floor. Perhaps this was the first monkey menace at school, which I had witnessed. Not only this, these creatures used to pop up anywhere to show their smiling visages, giving you the fear of the week! An incident I can clearly remember is when we came across one of our new teachers running in the corridor, shouting at the top of her voice, seeking help as she was being chased by a plump monkey who got attracted by the aroma of delicious food she was carrying in her bag!

There were teachers from all the states from the country, thus having nearly an equal ratio of north and south Indian teachers. All the teachers who taught us had a unique demeanor and were quite interesting. To name one, my science teacher whom I thought to be very strict; for instance, when I entered the class with a section allotment letter in my hand, I was scolded for being late, not even recognising the new face at that time. Later when she saw it and got to know that I was new to the school, she helped me adjust to the new school. Later on, I came to realise that she taught pretty well; her ability to have remembered the entire book, page to page was amazing! There were times when chapters like Diversity of Living Organisms, one of the most dreaded and lengthiest chapters of standard nine, could have been taught without opening the book for once, for even the sake of referral! Yet another eloquent teacher was our Hindi teacher, who always spoke in his fluent Hindi accent, not minding whether others, understood it or not! His passion for the subject made many of my classmates try and take on Hindi language in routine, although not so enthusiastically at first. Even my class teacher was very persistent as a Maths teacher. She used to put in the best of her efforts to make us adore Maths as one of the most sought-after subjects. Even though many had apprehensions regarding learning and practising Maths sums, she tried to keep the entire class engaged and attentive during the lessons. I still appreciate her efforts, remembering that she used to write questions and formulae all by herself to make our work and learning easy! I must be candid enough to disclose that my dedication towards Maths was generated here. I would see the parents of my classmates who were professors or faculty members in the reputed IIT Madras encouraging their wards relentlessly about the importance of doing well in Maths and Science subjects so that subsequently they got through the IIT entrance tests.

Studying in this school was an entirely new experience for someone like me who had never thought of speaking or understanding the language spoken here. From despising the school initially to later developing a liking to it, I took very little time to realise that it was just the cultural difference which I had not been attuned to. The children were the same everywhere, it was just that I did not care to know that before!

Chapter 8

THE EXAM FEVER DEADLIER THAN COVID FEVER?!!

I remember to have completed the paper in time and revised my answers twice. It was only then that I decided to put my head down and relax until the teacher collected the answer sheet. I was woken up by a loud resonant bell, which implied that the writing time was over, just then I turned over the answer sheets to check it for the last time and realised that I had missed solving the last part of the question paper. I could see the teacher literally snatching the answer sheets from all the students sitting in front of me and then … Goodness! It was a nightmare, of these kinds of evil dreams one sees a night before the exam day. It is not that you are unprepared, rather because you have fear of the later part, that is, the unknown 'result'. Exam days have always been a crucial transitional stage in a student's life when the person toils more than routine, inhibits self from indulging in hobbies

or anything other than studies in order to get good grades, which is considered the sole objective of pursuing education; I suppose from the experience I have had over the years! You can't bring yourself to think of the 'real and pertinent reasons' for conducting these dreaded assessments, that is, the exams! We normally forget that exams just test our knowledge and understanding of the concept taught and not us, per se!

The year 2020, my board year, gave me enough opportunities to write for these types of settings in order to sail through the 'most awaited' board exams. We were assessed after taking regular unit tests, monthly tests, periodic tests, quarterlies, half- yearlies, practice tests and finally the pre-boards, round the year! With all the kinds of exams available or discovered so far by our ancestors, we were prepared to face yet another exam, which differed from the rest in terms of difficulty, scale and the magnitude of fear and anxiety it generated. After all, it was conducted centrally by our board of education for lakhs of students like me studying in standard 10. However, our batch was ready to face something or 'everything' distinct from the previous years as the entire mode of learning was made online. This implied that we were no longer required to write the exams sitting in our worn wooden desks, under the direct supervision of our invigilators. But the year of online pedagogy, that is, 2020, assisted students to take the assessment from the comfort of their homes. And as the sports teams have a due advantage playing from their home turf with fans, predictability, known conditions and so on, the students too availed undue advantage of these home conditions with indirect or literally no supervision of our dear teachers!

Besides the pressure of the forthcoming exams, there was a heavy burden of assignments on us. We used to write for hours until our hands lost consciousness and gave up! The extremely tiring schedule of back-to-back classes and the assigned work left almost no time to relax. Although thinking of not completing the work could be thought of as an effortless option as the teacher did not know whether we were actually completing the work or using other smart methods but we used to be called to the school to submit our assignments' hardcopy, making us rush to the finish line! But the excitement of going to school after several months was severely disappointing when the aspect of submission of assignments was looked at with the hard and fast rules of social distancing which did not allow us to meet our friends, disrupting the main purpose of arriving at the rendezvous: our school! It was as if we had called someone over the phone and did not utter a word when the receiver was shouting "hello?"!

It was when almost half of the academic year was over when we were hunched over with the burden of completing the syllabus so that the rest of the year was spent revising and solving the sample papers efficiently, as planned by the planning commission of our school. So we were made to work hard to make the grade and our dear teachers used to inspire us by saying that our efforts would pay off for certain. And being a firm believer of the quote, "The more we sweat in peace, the less we bleed in war"; I gave more than a hundred percent persistent efforts of mine to ensure that I do not get nervous, run short of time, fail to answer and prepare for other contingencies and uncertain possibilities during the exams.

And it had never been present in my classmates, what is termed as the competitive spirit, which had started taking a toll on our friendship. I reminisce the moment when I had requested a 'long-lost' friend for the notes which had been shared in the class that I had missed as I was down with fever; she texted me, "Why don't you do it yourself? You seem to know everything, don't you? I regret but I can't share the work done in class today", with laughing emojis by the side. I had never imagined that my friend, who was the first one with whom I had come in contact while being new to the school, would turn her back when asked for help. But then I realised that I had misjudged and mistook her for a friend, who turned out to be jealous of my accomplishments. This competitive environment is as it is hard to live in, adding yet another reason to take stress; it was hard to believe the sudden change in some classmates' temperament; and that too because of the board examination competition in being.

The pandemic was enough to keep us strangled with uncertainty, fear and anxiety and now there were numerous other sources to keep us absorbed in negativity! I wholeheartedly hoped that the causal factors of stress were controlled and didn't trouble me further. In the midst of all this, we forgot to realise that the exams and acclimatisation to the new mode of school were insignificant issues to ponder over when we had the over-powering pandemic in the backdrop! It was enough to teach us to keep calm even in stressful settings.

Chapter 9

HALFWAY THROUGH THE BOARDS

Our evening class ended with a set of instructions regarding the forthcoming half yearly exams, which mark the end of half of the academic year. The major agendas of this prolonged online session were the protocols the students had to follow: students' integrity to refrain from indulging in any malpractice during online exams; instructions on abiding by the syllabus content; and the new marking policy for objective type answers. But only if my dear classmates obeyed the instructions! Instructions were followed by a lecture on general misconduct but I think that most of my classmates had muted the teacher's mike as no one, not even the teacher's dear disciples or the sycophants opened their mouths, to respond in approval. Perhaps, it was as if the teacher was the one asking and at the same instance, responding to the questions too. After uttering words like, "Is that clear?" or "Do you all agree with me?" and not getting any reply in the first half of the

session, she had given up the hope of asking for affirmation, later saying, "You all are intelligent enough to know what is wrong and right!" And I knew my class very well that they followed this maxim religiously that "If you obey all the rules, you will miss all the fun". I remember texting a friend asking her views about the ongoing lecture, which seemed to enthrall only the teachers, forcing students to take up other work for the time being. She answered, "Dude, Are you even listening to it? I had been watching YouTube for an hour now. You tell me if something important was said and I know you have nothing to say!" I broke into peals of laughter to acknowledge her reply. She was alright; no lecture could change the approach of the students while writing the exam, unless one is honest enough to not have a myopic view of the smaller gains, just to lose on the future board exams which were going to be offline only, in any case.

Online learning had forced the students to regularly adapt to practices that could have a negative impact on them, mainly due to lack of supervision by the teachers. A day before the half yearlies, one of my friends enquired about the syllabus of a subject. I was surprised to find the extent to which the levels of honesty had fallen during the pandemic. She was among one of the students, whose names flashed in the honour roll, scoring optimum marks in the quarterlies. Although we never found her answering any questions when asked by the teacher! She used to go blank or make an evidently fake excuse. That clearly implied that she had been cheating during the exams! Not only this, I was getting multiple calls during some of our exams, probably because Google didn't offer direct answers to the questionnaire and maybe our teachers had started adopting smarter ways to ensure that the concepts ruled over the cleverness of our folks, putting in indirect questions!

I remember the first time when I was made to learn the idiom 'honesty is the best policy', I was in standard one when almost the entire batch was compliant and ethical; and it was apparently the first idiom we had learnt but now the 'grown-up versions of those innocent law-abiding little fellows' just put it aside as if it does not have any meaning or essence. Yes, it is captivating to cheat and score marks that you are not worthy of but at the same time, working hard and achieving what you truly deserve is totally worthwhile. Over the years, I have observed my fellow classmates indulging in it as a result of peer pressure, high expectations of parents and teachers and most importantly their indolence! Furthermore, because of everything taking an online form, the pen-paper writing practices were also being endangered, assisting them to replicate the answers from the vastly knowledgeable engine, Google. Students were finding it handy to type or more precisely copy and paste the answers instead of writing them down. But amid this momentary joy, who would have cared to remember that the final exams were supposed to be held offline; on paper with a pen!

For me, it has always been awe-inspiring to write exams in a classroom, which has everything that an exam hall comprises of, that is, an invigilator, answer sheets, pin-drop silence and so on. But writing the exam at home is yet another intriguing experience as despite creating an artificial classroom out of your study room, not every aspect of an exam hall can be achieved. Nobody keeps looking at the examinees for the entire duration. And we were liberal enough to take a Kit Kat break even during the exam hours! The only criterion we need to really mind is handing in or forwarding the answer sheet at the right time!

The pre and post-exam phase always used to be a period, vividly restored in our minds, making us admire ourselves for working distinctly hard, at once! Needless to say, the exam day too, used to be either soothing or disturbing, depending upon the way we wrote the exams. Both the unforeseen sights clearly indicated our performance in the exam hall.

An incident I can clearly remember of is when we had to take an online English unit test and we were supposed to write a letter to the editor regarding a vexed issue; then an over smart boy of our class wrote to the editor similar to what was written in our workbook, not even slightly changing the Editor's address or the sender's address. So in the bargain, the receiver of the letter, that is, the Editor's address though remained The Times of India (similar to what was taught) but also the sender's address was C/O Mr. RK Sharma, Daryaganj, New Delhi, while we were in Chennai. Our English teacher read it aloud in the class, scolding him for not even using his brain while cheating!

This was an entirely new experience for us, beneficial only for the ones who remained as straight as a die! If we had been in school, we would surely have been given those extra five minutes that a few people always depend upon to fill in their answer sheets with last-minute answers. We all missed the school bell heralding the end of a particular exam and foremost the post-exam discussions about missing out the correct answer, someone forgetting the steps of the particular Mathematics question and many of us even applying the wrong formulae, making us prepared to face the music soon after! It used to absorb us discussing the answers of the exams like "It is 0.34", "No, it is 3.4"and one of us confessing later "I don't know how but my answer was 112". But we always used to console such friends by saying, "Don't worry, even steps fetch marks; so will you!" Those discussions were a source of unending fun for all of us, giving us a sense of relaxation after the mind-flexing exams!

All we can hope for is to get back to our schools, not only for exams but for enjoying those frolicking moments of bonhomie again!

Chapter 10

PTM

And the result of the half-yearly exams was announced in nearly a week. As this result was in no way a deciding factor for our promotion to the next class, hence with little or no excitement, we went through the mark list displayed on the school website. Some of the students had scored above average but to our surprise, most of us had clinched 'bounty'. Post the declaration of our results at the dreaded virtual Parents Teachers Meet or simply the *PTM*, we were well aware of the bittersweet truth that every one of us would be busted. Though the acronym for it has never been the same for students as they fondly refer it to *'Pitwayengi Teacher Mummy se'*, clearly implying the true connotation, as experiencing it themselves! At the school, it used to be one of the most serious days and we all were most articulate, extra courteous and sober – then. This day used to decide the quid pro quo behavioural conduct of the parents towards their child for the subsequent days! If our wishes could be horses, this fateful day would certainly have been blacklisted long ago!

But this parents teachers' meet was distinct from the usual ones; besides being virtual, it couldn't forge an experience of chaos created by parents, hurrying towards the respective classes, faces with serious and innocent looks of the children and happy facades of teachers ready to start in with their complaints which had been dormant in their minds for quite some time! But now it had nothing of such sort. All I could find was sectioned boxes with some technophobic parents, asking their wards about the commands; teachers being ready to present the screen and some video icons deliberately turned off. Perhaps this suggested that some children had joined while keeping parents at bay, not informing them about the scheduled meet. And they had decided to passively participate in the meet, portraying that their parents did not want to convey anything.

As our virtual PTM began, the class teacher started sharing the screen for the display of the mark sheet, simultaneously saying that almost everybody in the class had done well in the exams. She, including us, was surprised by the abrupt change in the graph of the performance of many; for instance, the ones who used to get 27 out of 80 had got 72 now! Although a change in attitude and hard work can be attributed to this change from 'a molehill to a mountain' charade, we were well acquainted with the extremely 'smart' children of our class who failed to make it look plausible! They should have kept this in mind that even graphs based on hypothetical situations don't show such a clandestine rise all of a sudden!

What followed was an hour-long lecture of our class teacher, focusing on how we should keep working hard and write our exams sincerely and honestly without supervision and mend our ways, not believing in any speculations coming our way, regarding the board exams. But speculations were there. Some popular ones were forwarded messages, which consisted of headlines like "Are the boards going to be cancelled?" or "No Board exams for the session 20-21?" And the most irritating part was the question mark, in the end, making us confused and unsure! As it is, students had considerably lost interest in studies due to indirect teaching techniques and dependence on self-learning methods and now with this, there were yet another set of unconfirmed reasons to assure them about their decision to refrain from some serious studying! But our teacher confidently put away all the doubts regarding this, starting yet another set of confidential speculations in our friend groups that she had a close link with the CBSE officials assigned for the job! But as the lecture progressed, it was evident that it was not paid heed by the children. Only the parents seemed to participate in the lecture that was mainly meant for students! And for making the lecture sound engaging, our dear class teacher gave an example of Arjun, a character in the epic Mahabharata, referring to his determination, the way he focused on his target that was the eye of the moving fish by seeing its reflection in the water, not anything else around and how we should follow that very maxim of being focused on our goal. At the mention of something other than studies, many students snapped back to attention. Surprisingly, some took it pretty seriously as a little later, on being asked about their aim in *life*, they remarked, "I want to pass class 10 with good marks!" That was obviously what everyone wanted, but as even the countries have perspective long-term plans and not just short-term five-year plans, the answer was notably astonishing and funny!

Once the boring and least anticipated lecture was over, we had an enthralling round of complaints by the teachers to dear parents. Another interesting aspect was our innocent response to the allegations made against each one of us as if we had nothing to do with them! And unexpectedly our teacher asked all the parents to give a confirmation for the students who had not turned on their videos or mikes for ages, that whether they genuinely had an irreparable issue or tested her patience by attending the class just for being marked present! Much to those children's dismay, this way ma'am failed to appreciate one of the ways adopted by them to fulfil the criteria of minimum attendance to get promoted to the next class! Another day when the attendance was being taken at the start of the class, nobody failed to shout 'Present ma'am' at the top of their lungs, but soon after many of them left the class or got affected by the plague of technical problems!

After the teachers were finished with their share, it was the time when the parents were given the opportunity to voice out their opinions and underlying doubts. One of the parents started by asking the teachers to set up a more difficult set of questions to ensure that students were given necessary exposure for the boards and also that no time was spent other than practising sums or referring to the boring reference books. And that was said so that we made the right use of the lockdown period. Obviously, listening to that made us feel uneasy and annoyed. Later that parent's ward had to issue an apology message seeking a pardon on our *Whatsapp* group for hurting the sentiments of almost all of his classmates!

Chapter 11

FESTIVITIES WITHOUT MUCH ADO

There has always been an environment of festivities during those pleasant days, normally starting from mid-September or early October when we are all usually done with our half yearlies and look forward to a fortnight of fun and frolic. It always used to be one of the most salubrious and awaited times of the year, with not much to study, owing to the exams that usually got over by that time! This ensured us a vacation that could be enjoyed to the fullest, with festive celebrations as icing on the cake! Even the idea of imminent festivals like *Diwali* and *Dussehra* could calm down the exhausting memories of the 'bygone exam days'!

India is a country known for a multitude of cultures and traditions accommodating harmoniously the needs of the vastly diversified nation and celebrating each of those fervent festivities with great enthusiasm. Though round the year, we are generally given holidays for all the festivals that show up whenever they are due but these routine breaks are only of a day or two. The awaited autumn break stretches up to more than a fortnight, rewarding enough pleasure and excitement throughout. However owing to the pandemic, the festivity fervour had been missing. We could no longer enjoy the vacation akin to the former ones. The restrictions and curbs had forcibly made it a low-key affair in each household.

Actually, *Dussehra* or *Vijayadashmi* is celebrated to mark the victory of good over evil as on that auspicious day, Lord Ram had killed the demon king *Ravan* and Goddess *Durga* had attained victory over the buffalo demon *Mahishasur* to restore and protect dharma. And *Diwali*, the festival of lights, is celebrated to commemorate the birthday of Goddess *Lakshmi*, the return of *Pandavas* post their banishment and the return of Lord *Ram* after defeating *Ravan*.

These accounts of mythical reasons for celebrating these occasions may bring reasons for festivities to elders, but we children always celebrated them to delight ourselves without understanding the faith and beliefs attached to them. I remember the last days of school before the autumn break every year when my classmates in the vicinity used to be busy making plans about the upcoming vacations. In the class, there used to be spirited rounds of talks consisting of conversations like; "Are you going out for the break this time or celebrating at home itself?" and if getting replies like; "Yes I'm going to the Maldives this vacay.", then the other envious ones, with replies on the contrast, used to quickly start in with their set of responses; "No, we'll be at home this time, celebrating the festivals in the way they are meant to be celebrated." And then the plane of conversation generally used to get complimented with infuriated outbursts and a pinch of evident sarcasm! On the whole, the excitement and enthusiasm used to charge us with a new burst of vigour.

And once the autumn break began, we used to find ourselves engaged in living those moments, which we keep writing down in our bucket list during routine days in order to motivate and invigorate ourselves, boosting the energy at least till the year end; through those lively junctures of life. But this pandemic made it lose its significance or the position it used to hold in the hearts of children as it was no longer awaited in such a way. This time, none of the other breaks made us feel elated. Rather, it was the longing to return to the normal life, with routine schooling, that rented the air of excitement in our mind. Remembering the winter vacations, those few authorised days of break always used to be extended by a week almost every year due to the district administration's order as the fog always crept up at the right time and for extended durations. Now it gives us a feel as if this lockdown, like a vacation of such sort, had been extended in a similar fashion. But the only difference the corona time exhibited was that it had no limits and nobody could estimate the limit of its existence; probably the entire year or maybe beyond!

These festivals meant get-togethers of friends and families, shopping for gifts and presents, lighting of the house with flickering *diyas* and bright luminous lights, cleaning and decorating of all the rooms, making of splendid *rangoli* designs at the entrance and also savouring of delicious cuisines,

exclusive of the festivals. At the same time, it also implied adorning ourselves with colourful ethnic attires. And this year, it consequently forbade a lot of people from updating their social media handles with their newly clicked pictures of the occasions as this time, the outfits were not *lehengas* or suits but comfortables worn at home! Though activities like cleaning and decorating the house could be possible even during the lockdown days, the true essence it held could not be matched as there could only be virtual family meets organised by some zealous children in the family! The way it used to bring all the members of the family together was a specialty in itself, giving a break from their usual schedule. Moreover, the lighting arrangements were also kept in small numbers. Besides, our empathy on seeing people suffering across the globe didn't allow us to enjoy the festivals like before.

Though the situation was still alarming, the daily infections had been reduced to some extent may be a result of us abiding by continuous precautions seriously. Keeping the spirit unabated, we decorated our house with lights and seeing the lights and all I could remember was the series arrangement of a combination of resistors; I had recently studied in Science. Such was the level up to which we had been engrossed in studies throughout and thus I was badly in need of that very break!

And then, I remember myself wearing new ethnic attire, bought online recently. I moved out of my dwelling straightaway to the opening that lay circular designs at a precise distance on both sides. After examining the *rangoli* I had decorated during the daytime, I shifted my focus to the broad sky. A thought struck my mind. I thought that this was going to be a year which would not have much adverse environmental impact, in terms of the air and noise pollution, the fireworks and crackers caused. But as soon as the sun set, I was surprised by the people all around as even then I could witness the spectacular array of lights and sound show in the sky.

And just then, one of my neighbours showed up, carrying a bag full of a variety of crackers. He had brought all of those for us as he had plenty of them for himself, having been sent from his native place, Sivakasi. It was heartening to see such a warm gesture, so I was told to crack a few of them, though entirely against my eco-friendly will! And luckily or unluckily, it had then started pouring, in its usual Chennai rainy setting, extinguishing all the *diyas* we had lit. But because of it, I was saved from polluting the environment in the ways I could! Thinking of the environment, I was catapulted into my school in the midst of a conversation wherein my classmates were discussing how it would have been outside our Science teacher's house as she had claimed of having planted a sapling every *Diwali*, thus sparking doubts of whether her house was surrounded by a forest by now!

Drifting back to the crackers and the town from where it was bought, that is, Sivakasi, it was known for firecracker, matchbox and big printing industries. These industries had employed over 2,50,000 people with an estimated turnover of Rs. 20 billion approximately. Huge indeed! This was popular across the world and until then, I had no idea about it. Thus with this, I got acquainted with one of South India's popular manufacturing unit's locations. And not only this, during this *Durga Puja*, falling around the autumn holidays, we 'windshield travelled' to witness the rich culture of South India while being in our car, with window glasses raised to its bar, to ensure safety. In our brief interaction with one of the locals, we found out that in Tamil Nadu, the festival of *Navratri* was called *Kolu*. It was celebrated in grandeur, marking the time when the women of the region set up decorated planks in a corner and placed on it all the dolls or *golu* on it in their houses. It was fun to learn about the culture and tradition prevalent here.

The festivities called on and went, making not much ado about anything; the main reason for it was the enthusiasm to meet each other but exuberance to organise such festivals were kept at low key amidst the precautions and protocols of the infectious disease. The only thing we wished for while paying obeisance to God on festivals this time was to restore life back to normal.

Chapter 12

WHAT.........! ARE YOU COVID POSITIVE?

B eing bone idle and having nothing to do, I thought of calling my best friend, Anjali who studied in the same standard as I did. We became best pals at the previous station, where my father was posted. And since then we were in touch with each other, despite being set afar. Talking to each other was one of our favourite pass times and we could gossip for hours until our phones really gave up! Moreover, it had been quite a long time talking to her, owing to the busy preparation schedule which the board exams had offered.

As I called her, she did not answer in the first instance. When I tried calling her again, I heard her utter in a feeble voice, evidently lower and distinct from her normal jovial temperament. I realised that something was amiss. On asking what the problem was, she revealed that she had symptoms like

that of COVID. Promptly, I asked in my usual teasing stature, "Anjali, c'mon you don't have to compare seasonal flu with coronavirus!" and later adding, "How can you get it? You always maintain precautions!" To which she wistfully narrated, "Dude, I haven't told you about this. Actually, my cousins, who stay abroad, came to India and called on our house a week ago. And since yesterday I feel sick and anxious, probably the symptoms are showing up now." Listening to her, I got the hang of the situation. Acting pragmatically, I asked her, "Why don't you get yourself tested then?" And much to my disbelief and dismay, she replied that her family was of the opinion of not getting the test done until the symptoms were vivid and testing was really required; probably all because of the fear of isolation and their social image. I could not believe that even educated people were falling prey to meaningless social stigmas about COVID-19!

Later I tried to convince her to persuade her parents for the same reasoning; they agreed to our plea. The moment I heard about Anjali's condition, I could not help my mind wandering away from work since then. I constantly remained concerned about her. And I had made sure, in my routine to call her at least twice daily to get updates about her health and keep her trepidation aside by engaging her in our usual hilarious conversations as much as possible. The aim was just to divert the unwarranted anxiety she had acquired in her mind.

During one of such calls, I got to know about her worries regarding her parents, who had multiple physical co-morbidities, thus exposing their vulnerability to the virus. Besides that, the incessant thought of the awaited results of the RT-PCR tests of her family occupied all parts of her brain.

Her anxiety was evidently audible in her voice. Probably it was the first time; I had seen her being so nervous.

It reminded me that after all, it was a super spreader pandemic, which had taught the entire human fraternity a big lesson, triggering a severe blow to the healthcare system of the entire world and affecting millions of people across. Apart from the increasing curbs, the advice on testing, preventive measures, management protocols, and even vaccination to tackle the highly infective virus was ever-expanding. So, the best I could do was to console her.

The following day, the results were known to us. Only she had tested positive for it and luckily the others did not. Subsequently, she was advised and made to stay in the outhouse, in isolation, since she had only mild symptoms and could recover at home itself. She was probably the first person so close to me, who got infected. I too used to be perturbed but tried my best not to divulge my anxiety in front of her. She was already suffering and could not afford to be mentally weak, and instead needed encouragement for her speedy recovery.

In haste, I made a *WhatsApp* group named 'Get Well Soon, Anjali', accommodating a bunch of concerned friends and her family members to ensure all the updates regarding her health were known to everyone. Later she was also added. Everyone posted text messages that had something to do with 'corona recovery', having all sorts of yoga asanas and breathing exercises prescribed for the purpose, meditation techniques, and generic medicines advised by the family doctor. The group usually had daily messages containing motivational quotes, owing to her apparent stress. And some members always made the group lively by dropping jokes and funny memes to keep her levels of anxiety low, at least for some time.

She did nothing other than watching television and reading novels, one of her favourite hobbies, for the first few days, but that could not last long. Admittedly, she was bored of those activities, and eventually, the loneliness was taking a toll on her mental health. I remember her, yelling in agony about her helplessness, which was beyond my imagination. The stress, internalised stigma, mental agony, fear of infecting kin, rewinding of events, realising the moment of contracting it, and her subsequent self-driven anger were not easy to calm and required lots of patience and empathy. During a video call, I found Anjali cursing her fate, saying, " Why is God punishing me?", adding her pain of remaining socially isolated from the family in a 'locked up' state was highly distressing.

All I used to say through these days was to not lose hope as everything would be alright soon. At the same time, her parents and sister also helped her providing everything she required and encouraged her to practice all breathing exercises and meditation techniques to maintain her ailing health. I, on the other hand, was there by her side, keeping her spirits high by mentally strengthening her. I used to say, "Dude, you should thank God for this, or you would have to be scared and nebulous about the infection like us, not knowing about it fully! You are fortunate to be asymptomatic to a large extent or you would have been kept in those corona wards with other patients you don't know and eventually unable to be in contact with us." I tried my best to help her forget about it, rather tried making her realise how beneficial her self-isolation was. I reminded her that she once used to yearn for freedom, away from her parents who kept scolding her, for her good although. With this, she also realised the importance of her friends and family and their significant roles in our lives. They are like fuel to our vehicles, who keep us going. To divert her mind and bring her back on track, I shared a few worksheets, saying, "You are recovering now, so better start studying, our boards would not wait for you!" Although she could not concentrate like before, she could at least drift back to her normal life which swung around studies! With adequate rest, she had begun studying, eventually pushing away her troubling thoughts of the COVID infection.

After 14 tough days of isolation and recovery, her test results came out to be negative. On hearing the breaking news, I was extremely delighted as if I was the doctor who showed her the path to recovery! It was probably the first time in those dreaded days that she laughed wholeheartedly, making us realise that her 'true self' had returned from a fortnight of exile!

This period of 'real test' proved to be more difficult than the ones we always face. The novel coronavirus made the isolation period seem like a solitary exile for many. From my experience, the feeling of knowing about the status of someone's recovery is more satisfactory when you have lent even a small help towards making it feasible!

Chapter 13

As if Corona Was Not Enough!

It was pouring cats and dogs that day when I heard the beep-beep sound of my phone, indicating a *Whatsapp* notification. I turned around to fetch my phone to find that the classes for the subsequent days had been suspended due to the terrific cyclones that had been predicted by the meteorological department in the state. The prevalent fake excuses that continued to keep our classmates devoid of any admonishments from the teacher like power cut, no internet connection and other innovative explanations appeared to be taking reality and sensing the same even our school administration had declared the closure of the classes for some indefinite period.

As I got to know about the news, I sighed to digest the information about the new bomb that had been thrown away

at us; all of a sudden. It appeared favourable for me to ponder over the situation, which by no means seemed fine. After all, it is obvious to feel uneasy, thinking about the calamities that stood just a stone's throw away. It was as if the fast-replicating virus and lockdown were not enough to ravage the fear of the grief-stricken masses of the country that storms and cyclones of various intensities and different names had come to make and wreak havoc now.

I remember the TV screens flashing something other than that of viral casualties. The headlines in trend also seemed to be equally fatal, complementing the already built stress. But in no time, we could also be reassured, seeing our efficient disaster relief workers swinging into action. The safety alerts had been issued everywhere so as to accrue minimum damage, in terms of life and property. That meant building temporary shelters for people who needed to be displaced from the vulnerable areas. But at the same time, that could also involve many people crowding, exposing them to the viral infection. In a nutshell, it was a difficult time for those poor people, who seemed to get affected by either of the causes, anyway!

Strict instructions were issued to maintain requisite safety and security protocols during the natural calamity. And I thought that it was a déjà vu; later realising that I had read about these situations several times in my textbooks and now was going to experience the severity of a cyclone in person. Theoretically, it was supposed to be a very severe rapid inward circulation of air masses around a low-pressure centre, but with my information, gathered from news and eye witnesses, I could only find that the cyclone, *Nivar* was accompanied by threateningly destructive stormy weather. Many trees outside my house had surrendered and laid unconscious on the roads, giving an altogether different sight of the acquainted road. *Nivar*, the horrifying phenomenon, made its landfall over north coastal Tamil Nadu between Puducherry and Chennai, at some of the areas of Andhra Pradesh and in Sri Lanka.

Looking outside through the windows, we could feel the magnitude of the havoc created by it and assume the situation in the areas on the eastern coasts, exposed for its extremity. And as many trees had fallen in my neighbourhood, strangling the electric poles with live wires, it had been difficult to venture out even to observe the area. We could see our lawn flooded up to two feet, leaving no way to step out. It had also become a breeding ground for the mosquitoes, making us susceptible to yet other health hazards like dengue and malaria, besides the coronavirus and exposure to the cyclonic conditions, of course! It felt as if nothing could have been worse!

There was a power cut too and we could not expect it to be restored anytime soon due to the evidently disrupted electrical lines. So I was perched in my hammock, which was put in the verandah. I kept looking indulgently at the gushing water at the near confluence of the drain. It was as if water was flowing downstream, which could be felt from my house located at a height than the other surrounding areas. The continuous flowing of the contaminated water seemed to continue for hours, making me feel that I lived on the bank of a feisty river. This was one of the very few times when I had no apprehensions sitting out in the abruptly not-so-hot turned weather, doing exactly nothing. I always preferred to sit inside, but that day our battery inverter too had packed up, leaving us dependent on emergency lights and natural illumination. Having nothing to do, I remembered the good old days of the previous year when everything was in place, from the social interactions, schools, evening games or the countryside holidays. It was only then I remembered that when there used to be a power cut at the school, we could hear many remarking, "The light went!" as if the light departed for some new place or "There is no light!" and the teacher used to reply, saying that there are no such expressions, correcting them by saying, "There's a power cut!" What fun it used to be in the 'old' normal with no viruses and cyclones striking!

Some days later when the intensification of the cyclone had been depreciating, the news channels could be seen with another name flashing: *Burevi*, yet another cyclone. Seeing that, the first thought that sprung to my mind was that who was the one naming these annoying cyclones! And only later did my parents told me that it was done to simplify communication between forecasters and the general public regarding forecasts and warnings. These names were intended to reduce confusion in the event of concurrent storms in the same basin. To name a few cyclones, I could remember were *Amphan, Tauktae, Yaas*; except for their name nothing was beautiful about them, with mainly destruction as their mandate. But fortunately the weak tropical cyclone *Burevi* passed without much destruction or making us feel the impact, maybe because we had experienced something akin to it, but of more intensity. With the fortnight of back-to-back cyclones, we breathed a sigh of relief to find that no 'new' cyclone was due sometime soon! And we drifted back to the recently adapted new normal life of pandemic.

A remarkably horrifying time throughout the year we had spent with severe cyclones like *Burevi, Nivar and Amphan*, which kept calling on to the Indian coastal areas and shores.

These situations forced a large number of our population to be evacuated, sheltering protocols to minimise COVID spread. But lately, I came to realise that such cyclones or deluges were actually testing times of the human perseverance which was already challenged with the unresolved pandemic.

Chapter 14

THE SHOT OF HOPE

Probably 2020 was the first year in which I literally did not go anywhere. This statement has clearly no exception or 'ifs and buts' as I did not even go to school, where I used to be present on almost all the days except holidays! Actually, I was not the only one who had experienced this; there were lakhs of people who had spent the entire year like me, in utter confinement at home. There was no unnecessary venturing out. All this had been made possible because of the deadly virus, of course!

From curbs to lockdown, routine screening of active cases, fatalities and fear of uncertainty; we have experienced it all. But after all, life is all about ups and downs. Though this time the troughs had been pretty low and frequent, we had a few crests or peaks too. Obviously, the crests symbolise the 'few good times' and troughs the 'many bad ones' we had spent throughout the year and I firmly believe that every day may not be good but there is something good in every day. Thus even if most of the year was dull, there were a few rays of bright light which gave us a sense of silver linings towards the end of this pandemic in near future.

With little or no celebrations, we bid adieu to 2020, the year of coronavirus. Nothing else can be attributed to that year. Like every year I had planned to have New Year's resolutions and those were about the changes that I had considered bringing in me, as such resolutions are generally self-driven and not embarked. The resolutions ranged from developing gratitude towards everyone to working relentlessly harder to pursue my dreams. And my wish list contained just one point; 'the pandemic should be over soon'. All these rituals had not been much different from those of the previous years. However, I knew that like the resolutions, the approach and priority towards their fulfilment would be the same, abiding by them to an extent only. But this time I made it a point that I would not crib about the situations or take endless stress, rather I would try to practise and promulgate the idea of hope and willpower in trying times like these. For a pandemic-struck population that was desperate for revival against the virus, the most optimistic projection was regarding vaccine or inoculation shots that were supposed to be ready by the year 2021's beginning. The speed at which those shots were developed and rolled out was a remarkable achievement, marking the country's great scientific feat.

And to support my maxim of hopefulness, the government assured that the vaccination drive would begin in January. This ushered in a new hope, providing a sense of respite. People

across the globe had been waiting for the vaccine impatiently as until then there could not have been any other solution for the viral infection, exposing the vulnerability of the masses. Perhaps it came to be considered as the 'shot of hope'. And we were ensured that people of certain age groups would be administered the shot of hope in our country, first; and later the drive would expand, covering other age groups too.

But now the irony of the situation was that a lot of people had apprehensions regarding vaccination, which was once the most sought after and needed solution! We could hear and read about even the educated people believing in myths and speculations about the vaccines. One of the most popular myths was that these shots were not safe as they were made in haste! But people believing and not wanting this would have been the ones criticising the policymakers and pharma industries if the vaccines had not been developed. Rather, they should have complimented their efforts to have come up with the solution so fast, which normally would have taken years if the normal pace would have been followed! Moreover, other established myths regarding the same were that people inoculated would develop severe COVID-19 symptoms and the ones already infected do not need vaccines. I know how it feels to know these reactions of people who believe and spread the wrong word, failing to recollect the principle on which immunisation is based! Disheartening indeed. Yet another 'celebrated' myth was that the person, who had been fully vaccinated, did not require wearing masks and following protocols. As if the individual had become invincible! Also, there were forwarded messages from people about vaccines that they had side effects and caused allergies. Those people participating in the 'forwarding chain' had such strong conviction against its usage as if they were present while the vaccines were getting manufactured and their testimonies regarding the materials used could help save the world from 'vaccine virus' and thereby they would be felicitated with Nobel Prize for their services offered! Consequently, many people got to believe these myths and remained sceptical about getting vaccinated. Furthermore, it was their loss only as we Indians did not have a treasure full of doses. And if adults had such beliefs, there was hardly any chance that they would let their beloved children get inoculated.

Aforesaid, we all would not be surprised to know and agree upon the sources and mediums for these myths to traverse along the country—the mediums of mass communication. Our 'favourites', the social networking sites made the transmission of this 'virus of myths' possible, to a greater extent.

Also, the fear of getting infected and further infecting our family kept us absorbed in the thick air of anxiety and fear. We had unwillingly become 'self centred', not the correct description though; but not that irrelevant either. Assisting others in need did not mean going and attending to COVID patients and in turn, getting infected, rather it meant succouring the ones we could, like feeding stray animals, paying domestic helps even if they were not able to render services, donating stuff to needy and so on. There were myriad activities we could think of while lending our helping hand to people in distress.

We were all fed up with the coronavirus and concerning that, many other variants of these 'viruses' came into being subsequently. But these viruses, I am mentioning, were not submicroscopic bodies; rather they were marked with our tendency to forget our innate virtues like humanity, compassion and hope. For corona the vaccine was insight but for our souls, the 'shot of hope' is still missing.

Chapter 15

A Window of Relief

With the beginning of the year 2021, there was hope for things to get better since the statistics indicated that the number of daily cases had reduced to a large extent. But that did not necessarily mean that the virus and its impact were going to disappear suddenly. Although the situation was not worth making merry, it had not become worse either. Actually, with vaccinations and decreased daily infections, we could breathe a sigh of relief, finding ourselves being led to a better situation. It was also the time when we had also started to imagine ourselves out of the pandemic scenario.

As the year commenced, there was a new hope that we would someday be able to live a life of pre-pandemic days without masks, social distancing and not fearing of viral infections! During one of such days, when the daily cases were too less to worry about, my family made a plan to have a trip down south, while following the COVID protocols providently as we would probably not be able to take a tour of that axis in near future, owing to our busy schedule and decrease in proximity to these areas in times to come.

I have more or less seen most of the parts of the country, courtesy of being an army kid; because of the frequent postings and also our tours and excursions which we would definitely plan once or twice every year. But all this could be a compulsory fixture only before the pandemic. However, these trips' timings would mostly match my availability, in terms of my exam schedule or school calendar. But the year 2020 left us in a lurch to better care for safety than leisure. Once the guidelines for COVID were relaxed by the Government authority and the tourist agencies were given a go to operate, we also found a reason to celebrate. A quick plan followed. My father is known for executing such flexible no-time plans. As per him, we should always live life to its fullest, work and study hard and party even harder.

The busy schedule of class 10 was not going to spare me easily, so in order not to miss out on significant lessons or revision schedules, we made sure to utilise the brief break post the pre-boards for our tour. Thus after the exams were done away with, I did not spend my time resting or talking to friends like I always did, rather this time I engaged myself in helping my mom packing for the tour. This was probably one of the few times when I was involved in it as neither did I show any interest in doing this job nor were my parents confident of my skill on it. But this time none of those excuses could help me as neither did I have to prepare for exams nor did a generous friend show up at the right time, asking for my company! So I had to stuff in all sorts of things, ranging from clothes to shoes to my autograph diary. After all, we could have run into a celebrity!

Once the packing and other arrangements were over, we set out for our road trip, fully prepared to be safe. We started our journey early in the morning for the island town of Rameshwaram situated at the southeastern tip of the Indian peninsula. It was going to be an 8-hour long drive, all the way to the temple town. I did not know much about Rameshwaram until the day before when we all had been preparing the tour itinerary. All I knew was it being the native place of our former president and the missile man of India. An aerospace scientist and inspiration for many, Dr. APJ Abdul Kalam, was born and brought up there. I was going to witness that teeming small island town, which was venerated because of his divine presence. And I wished to seek his omnipotent blessings and preaching, whilst being there. But now that I had done some research, I could guess what I was going to witness as far as the other attractions were concerned.

During all the car journeys I had so far, I used to be very enthusiastic initially but very soon I used to get exhausted and would subsequently find myself dozing off. But at this time of the hard-earned excursion after the life in lockdown which was lived within premises, every bit of outside, be it roads, countryside, landscapes seemed extremely picturesque and enchanting. But sooner or later I got into my syndrome of dozing off in the comforts of the big car, comfortable cool AC circulation and the driving skills of my father. It was after sometime, that I was woken up with exclamations of observing the beauty of the surroundings by my dear mother who even insisted me to watch the 'surreal' in front of us. I struggled to look at my mother, who was taken aback by the beauty of the bridge in front. I tried to open my eyes, only to find that we were on the famous Pamban Bridge, a railway bridge and the only channel that connected our destination with mainland India. It was not just a connecting link but also a location worth stopping by. It was India's first sea bridge and thus obviously had spurring bluish-green seawater, maintaining its awe and beauty. The engineering state of the artwork was a marvelous piece to be watched in real.

Reaching Rameshwaram, we could feel the tranquility of the peaceful temple city. The moment we got there, we checked in our hotel and rested until the following day dawned. We spent our day at Ramanathaswamy Temple, which is considered to be one of the holiest temple destinations of Hindus, and also a part of the Char Dham pilgrimage. Consequently, we were off to Dhanushkodi, which was an abandoned town at the south-eastern tip of Pamban Island. It was literally the 'last piece of land' belonging to the sovereign Indian territory. It was vacated post a cyclone that destroyed much of it, leaving it in ruins. The national highway which led us to the last point suddenly 'ended' when there was literally no place to go forward. It was an awe-inspiring experience to see the southeastern tip of the Indian peninsula.

After enjoying our sojourn at Rameshwaram, we headed to Kanyakumari which is literally the 'land's end' or 'Cape Comorin', as we call it, the southernmost point of the mainland. On the way, when we neared Kanyakumari I was mesmerised to see the windmills that were far too many, along the road; having read about these in geography to seeing them myself, was a great moment. The drive and serene beauty of the place added with the presence of these windmills reminded me of the hinterland of Netherlands; yes that beautiful it was! But seeing them moving continuously was hypnotising and astonishing for me. I began to wonder about the energy generated and put to use by their rotation, there were so many as if the whole of South India's electricity production was taken care of by these windmills! And also that India would have been the leading country to have so many of them!

After the tiring journey of around 6 hours, we halted at our stop. We hit our bed the moment we reached it as we did not want to miss the sunrise the next morning, which was one of the key attractions of the place. Seeing the sun making its presence felt from the cloak of the concealing clouds was worthwhile! Starting the day with witnessing the natural phenomenon, we set out for the twin tourist attractions, the famous south Indian poet Thiruvalluvar's statue and Swami Vivekananda's rock through a ferry. The location and the long-built architectural wonders were spectacular! And in the evening, we witnessed the sunset on the same beach, making it the only place to witness the sun's arrival and departure from the same location. Visiting the land where the three huge water bodies, that is, the Bay of Bengal, the Arabian Sea and the Indian Ocean meet was an amazing experience in itself!

At last, when our tour of four days was approaching its end, on the way back to Chennai we headed to Madurai, our last destination. Midway, I keenly observed salt farming which was taking place all around the road, from letting it dry to filtering. It was fun to watch the process on the ground; whatever I had read in my course book. I wonder whether it was my parents' plan to help me locate all the industries of Tamil Nadu I had uninterestingly read about!

We had specifically made a plan to visit Madurai, only to pay our obeisance at the Meenakshi Amman Temple. Besides the religious importance it held, its architectural artworks were yet another display of richly sculptured south Indian temples. It was so magnificent that I could hardly behold such a view with my awe-struck pair of eyes!

In a word, the tour could evidently be described as relaxing, especially away from the world of tensing reality! But there was one thought that was constantly in my mind, "Now that I had relaxed for a week, I would have to study for pre-boards 2!" And thus, I drifted back to my busy schedule of board preparations once again.

Chapter 16

BACK TO BENCHES: COURTESY PRE-BOARDS

My mother happened to be one of the core group members of the 'Teachers and Parents' Group' and that is why I was the first few to be privy to the School and Board's decision regarding the conduct of pre-boards, to be in the offline mode. Yes! I was super excited to have found a reason to meet friends, speak our minds in person, crib, feel happy and talk endlessly as it used to be before.

But perhaps it was not going to be the way we thought of it. The thrill of the first message did not last long as we failed to realise what our Principal was still 'typing'. The italicised word 'typing' meant that the message was incomplete and there was something more in store for us. This bouncer was fast but predictable enough to force us to dodge at the right time. What followed was the list of instructions and protocols we mandatorily needed to follow at school. We had to refrain from all the 'once daily' affairs like hugging, shaking hands, sharing tiffins and staying close by. And along with it was another ruthless instruction received as a text message that stated that the ones who failed to comply with the aforesaid measures would be punished and suspended. So the notice cum warning turned out to be something we had already expected, but not to the extent of severity it mandated.

One of my friends suggested, "It is alright if we would not be allowed to mingle in school. We can meet outside school, can't we? After all, they cannot put a tracking device behind each one of us!" Such were the ideas prevalent in our 'socially distanced' minds. But later we realised that following this, actually we would not be cheating our dear teachers but ourselves, for our selfish exuberant acts might put ourselves as well as our family's health at stake.

Going to school, although just for the duration of exams, required all of us to swing back to a life of pre-pandemic days. These exams were also going to be the first 'real' tests at school as most of our teachers had hardly imposed faith in our online test performances for doubts of having copy-pasted answers in the virtual answer sheets. Many of our classmates knew that they would be exposed, thus burning 'midnight oil' was the only option left to them and that too on short notice. The stress in the offing could make them go nuts!

As the day for the first 'offline' exam came calling, I struggled to wake up early, having been used to getting up late during the online classes regime. I rushed to get ready, not knowing where the 'long forgotten' school uniform had taken refuge. After having searched for nearly half an hour, I remembered the location where it had been transferred to, post laundering the stains of those bright colours. Once the dots were connected, I realised that I had celebrated Holi, wearing my uniform on the last day of our exams, months ago. That was the last day of the pre-pandemic normal schooling fixture. Now the next task was to locate the shoes and socks, which once used to be in pair, always together! Once I had been done with all this, I headed for the last minute revision before going to school; the checklist of ensuring nothing had been missed for the exam and above all the 'musts' like mask, sanitizer, handkerchief, geometry box, exam board and so on. Finally, my parents set out to drop me at school as my school bus was not plying then.

Lo and behold! We had to make a U-turn as we moved out some miles ahead of our home, suddenly I exclaimed, "Oh no! I forgot to take my identity card." The reactions of my parents were self-explanatory, leaving nothing for me to say other than those magical apologetic words, "So Sorry". So once again we made our way towards my school after tracing and taking my identity card, the document that permitted us to enter the IIT Campus.

Apart from the words used for seeing me off, my mother said, "You need to be very careful at school and for God's sake, do not indulge in any activity against the COVID protocols. You are old enough to understand that. Take care and good luck!" Listening to the precaution, I thanked her and bid her bye. I knew that I had to do what I was supposed to.

I headed to the school gate to find all the tenthies, the only ones among all the students of the school, called to take the examination waiting to get in. I was fascinated to see the faces of my friends though masked, still beaming. We could make out the expression, the others wanted to convey. The next moment, we got into a line that was marked with boxes placed at one-meter distance from each other. And there were two levels we had to pass through, before walking in the school corridor. Firstly, one of our staff members stood, with a handheld thermometer gun, to ensure none of us were feverish or symptomatic. Then we had to pass through a semi-circular passage that disinfected us, spraying liquid sanitisers over us. I was amazed to see all that, none of which had been present before, like this COVID.

Not only the 'receiving ceremony', but our school premises also seemed different. It was not because we were there after ages, but the school walls now looked different, duly adorned with caricatures of students, advising us to follow all COVID SOPs. The boxes, separating two of us with six feet distance, one after the other, led us to our exam hall. But I must confess, none of us failed to utilise the opportunity of talking while making our move through our respective boxes. Unlike the routine strength that could easily be accommodated in our spacious classrooms, only 15 students were made to sit in each room. The desks that we once used to climb over to reach to one another were placed at a distance, obviously inhibiting such activities.

We took our seats and found the blackboard in front was all clear as if dusted well and waiting for me, the 'Class Prefect' to come forward and write the details of the present strength, absent state, subject and the class teacher's name at the top right corner, followed by writing some of our classmates' name in the centre, who would make noise. Everything around seemed to have changed, we got to know from our teachers that even the monkeys had stopped coming to pay their visits, perhaps unable to find kids and their share of foods to excite them for!

We began writing the exam as soon as the bell made a known resonant sound. I could see some of my classmates trying to grab the attention of one another as the facial expressions could no longer help them notice that someone required their help, owing to the masks that shielded and suffocated us. It was one of such endeavours by our dear friend to seek 'help' when our invigilator noticed him trying to cough unnecessarily, seeking attention. Right then, he was shown a yellow card, making him aware of the fact that another mistake would ensure him a penalty of marks! But being habitually forced, he committed the sin again and the teacher came forward with her dreaded red pen to write a remark. Like always, he started pleading, "Ma'am, I am very sorry. Please forgive me. I would never repeat this mistake." And she responded curtly, saying, "You have not been called to the school to exhibit all this, better be at home and continue your job." So at last, akin to the regular amnesties on such accounts, he was spared for the last time as he promised to bring a letter, the one signed by his parents! This surely reminded us that though this pandemic had changed the mode of living but not the essence of exams and some regular incidents we used to cherish.

After the answer sheets were collected, we rushed to take our bags and also to keep up with the old tradition of our discussions and the good, bad and ugly comments on the question paper! But as soon as we started, we were obstructed with a high shrill sound of our sports teacher's whistle; perhaps he had been assigned to look after the social distancing norm among students! And we were forcibly let out of the school, in the same line we used to enter. Also, the idea of talking outside the school had to be called off as teachers were present even outside to make sure that we head straightaway towards our parents and in safe hands.

As said earlier, all other exam days went off in a similar fashion, preventing our interaction to a great extent. But whatever it was, the sense of at least getting to see our friends and stepping into our classrooms was more than satisfying. Hoping for something that was inevitably practical; enjoying like usual, was not wise.

Chapter 17

The Final Pursuit to Excel

Now that all the practice papers planned by our school including the formal pre-board exams had been conducted, online or offline, we were given a 2-month long study leave in which we had to do nothing but prepare for the board examinations due in May 2021. This was unusually late as per the CBSE schedule, but the COVID curbs had forced the policymakers to come up with such a decision.

But all this did not mean that we were given time for mere introspection or validation of our thoughts. Rather, it meant that we had to work exceptionally hard for the D Day. We had to spend most of our study period at home, studying, solving sample papers, revision sheets, and previous years' questionnaires, time management tests, and so on; to sail through with the best results in the board exams. On the last day before the study leave, we had to attend a strategic meeting which had the presence of all our subject teachers, ready to assist us. They assured us that they would help the ones in need, even during the self-study period. Rather than being obliged for their welcoming generosity, we were all surprised to find the importance the boards had, such that all our respected teachers were ready to walk the extra mile with us even when we were supposed to travel solo! Panic-stricken, we marched forward, keeping our spirits high, towards the last schedule of the academic year before the final countdown.

We were given timetables to adhere to or derive ideas to make a perfect study routine before the dreaded boards. Deliberately or not, we had to put the regime, assigned by our teacher in order to cover all the topics in time. It stated that we had to start our day studying and even end it whilst engrossed in studies! How tedious it was! I knew it was not going to be easy but I had to make sure that I achieved my goal of getting a high average percentile. Though being quantitative and attaining high percentile or numbers should not be the aim but setting up a goal for yourself will make the journey worthwhile and meaningful, I believe.

The prolonged study, inhibiting us from indulging in any other activities had taken a toll on our mental health, giving us enormous stress for the offline scheduled mass level examination: 'the Boards'. When we were studying for almost entire non-sleeping hours of the day, we used to find many others, particularly children in other standards, trying to kill the boredom of quarantine by watching some OTT platform content, as heard. But, we tenthies were deprived of all of that stuff, from watching IPL to even playing games!

Amidst the study period, I regularly complained to my mother about having an immense headache. Subsequently, I was taken to an ophthalmologist as my mother suspected me of having myopia, listening to all other symptoms that I constantly repeated in a painful voice. And much to my dismay, the eye specialist handed me a prescription stating that I needed glasses! That was something I never really wanted, but then I was forced to give up my reluctance to wear it, thinking of making that small sacrifice that could help me study without any discrepancies. Initially, I tried to reason with my mother, saying that I could see far and wide even without those concave pieces of lens but my plea was easily put down as after all I could not ignore those difficulties I faced in doing my work. I used to get accompanied by a bad headache whenever I parted ways with my glasses. Actually, it was my misconception of not wishing to portray myself as a nerd, wearing those big glasses all the while! And since then I have been consuming all sources of Vitamin A and other supplements to get rid of it.

When we were almost there, waiting for days to pass and the date of the 'boards' to dawn, it seemed that everything had stopped. It was as if we had to continue that 'hard on us' study routine time and again, the way we had been doing for the past one and a half years, being stuck in the same class, because of the pandemic though. But time flew as it had to. The nation witnessed a surge in the number of infections and fatalities as a result of COVID-19. A new variant of the virus was found and its effect was simply devastating, calling for wider and more concerns than ever. And in the midst of this, there were rumours on social media that board exams were going to be called off soon. That had become one of the trendiest talks in the environment, actively involving common masses and iconic personalities with their concerns on various social media platforms about the kids, who could be exposed to the vulnerability of the virus. People tried to reason with the government to come up with different alternatives that could prevent lakhs of students from exposure to the deadly infection. The foremost concern of the parents of the 'tenthies' was their wards' safety. Apart from that, they also did not want a year to be wasted like that. And all this accounted for such a debate!

With so much uncertainty and doubt, I tried my best to focus sincerely on the board exams, leaving the decision of postponing and cancellation of the conduct of the exams to the authorities who could make a difference in taking the decision. But in the midst of all this, we matriculates were in the dilemma of whether to continue preparing for the boards or leave and start something new! As it was, a long time had been spent reading, writing and revising the same books multiple times, just to seek perfection in the board exams! But then we did not know what to do, seeing many people voicing their concerns over the boards and thus remained doubtful until the last day.

The anxiety mainly arose due to some unanswered questions like: are the boards going to be called off? If yes, then should we consider revising the same old syllabus? And if no, then should we derive anything from the much believable speculations that have been doing the rounds?

Chapter 18

AND IT HAPPENED: EXAMS CANCELLED!

April 2021 onwards, I used to wake up early, owing to the ensuing board exams drawing near. The environment during the exam time used to be very different at my home front. Strict discipline, timetable, assured leisure time and of course, lots of pampering used to be the order of the day. Early to bed and early morning studies gave me tremendous confidence while revising the subjects, as it used to help me enhance my concentration grip. Despite the air of rumours and talks regarding the cancellation, I had made up my mind to study until the 'news' came from verified sources. So I tried my best not to be influenced by any of that hearsay propaganda.

It was 14 April 2020 and 1400 hr to be more precise when the final proceedings of the conference were under progress regarding the fate of the board exams. Even our honourable Prime minister was a part of the meeting. Many affected parents were glued to the news channels. Even I told my mother to keep a tag of it. But like always she told me, "You don't worry, keep working hard; these are board exams and thus will never get cancelled. Yes! They will be postponed, keeping up with the corona situation and a window will be there when things will happen." Such motivational parlance was used to keep me going. On that note, even this was another usual day for me.

And according to the rigorous set timetable, I was supposed to solve sums from the RS Aggarwal Maths reference book, the one whose thickness resembled the Oxford dictionary and such size could make you despise Maths! When I was in the midst of solving a question, mingled with $\sin\theta$s and $\cos\theta$s; I saw the notification centre of my phone getting flooded with messages, being marked by the continuous ringer sound. I checked my phone to find that all groups and personal chats contained messages stating "The board exams for standard 10 stands cancelled for the year 2020-21". Initially, I thought it was like any other rumour bug, which was continuing to make people believe something unnecessary. Later, I realised that not everyone would suddenly be plausible to such speculations, thus I thought of leaving everything and discerning the truth. Our official class *Whatsapp* group too contained that news with our teachers nodding in confirmation. This 'news of the day' was welcomed with reactions like 'Wow', 'Thank God' and 'let's party' or on the contrary 'Why?' and 'That can't happen', thus inviting mixed responses. The funniest part that followed this was that a boy of our class had mistakenly posted

happy emojis, clearly conveying his happiness, in the official group. However, he had to delete the message immediately as just a few days ago he had been given a long lecture for mending his ways.

But in my case, the moment I got the news, I could not understand whether to continue solving those questions or just leave it midway. I set aside the thick book. Seeing it reverentially, I realised that probably it would not be required soon unless I really wanted to solve that. I looked at my mother, she was as confused and shocked as I was; maybe because even she had been toiling hard in helping me all through these days.

I was rather unhappy with the decision because I had worked extremely hard for the 'previously' anticipated board exams. Had I known that the exams were going to be cancelled, I would not have studied so much. By that time, I was confident enough to explain all the concepts without even referring to the book, courtesy of my exam preparations! It was as if our relentless efforts would not be paid off. But besides being unhappy with the 'unexpected' decision, I was relieved to find that now I would not have to toil hard for some days, at least. And even the rumours of ambiguity would not surround me any further. After all, I realised that it was all for our safety's sake, if not lakhs of matriculates would have been vulnerable to the new variants of the virus. This would have put the nation's future, that is, the youths, in peril.

I can vividly recollect the expressions of some acquaintance pretending to be a well-wisher, considering us 'lucky' to have missed out on the dreaded examination by saying, "Oh, how lucky! You would not have to write those difficult exams." My friends and I, who mistakenly happened to get into that fatuous conversation, responded to that, saying, "Being lucky is not missing out on the boards, rather being safe. And coming to classifying our 'luck', who would have been more unfortunate than us to work and not get the desired results?" This had become the 'most talked about' issue among commoners, with their views about our 'luck' taking a storm of opinions!

Apart from that, we were also unclear about the promotion criterion and specifically 'our future', which appeared 'virally bleak, because of the virus'. We had no idea that the yearlong break from physical school would extend further, perhaps dissipating much of our existing school life!

Putting everything aside, I decided to relax as thinking unnecessarily about something that had become a past thing by then would be nothing but a waste of time. So I utilised that very day talking to all my friends who had also been given that rare privilege of 'being promoted to the next class without appearing for the boards'!

While I was busy talking, subconsciously, my attention used to divert to the wall clock, reminding me of getting back to my study table; that was the level of my sincerity during the preparation of the bygone board exams. The cancellation of exams could not give me the requisite feeling that I had passed that class and was pushed into a break before the new academic year. Whatever I was doing, I felt that the next thing I would do was to study. And for the subsequent days, I felt that

I was missing out on usual studies for long hours! Such mental shift needed to be familiarised.

And remembering those days, while I was still busy preparing, I used to yearn for relaxation and wanted to be in a book-free zone! But now I was beginning to miss that, not because I loved fretting for it, but mainly because the long study hours had become a routine since the lockdown schooling of standard 10 began.

And I must confess, the break post cancellation of the board exams was wonderful. I could literally do the things which were part of my bucket list. I readily agree with the fact that the sight of the same old books used to make me fed up while I was still onto it! But now that we 'matriculates', having been set free from the one-and-a-half-year of staying in the same class, were more or less contended to explore the underlying future possibilities!

It was only during those relaxed times, a forced sabbatical after the gruesome hardworking days, when I reflected "why not to write my experiences of the year that was; about pandemic time and our hopes, fight or fright amidst the preparations for board exams". I thought of writing about the "history which our batch, the 'corona matriculates' had created by passing the board exams without even appearing for it".

Chapter 19

HAD CORONA NOT BEEN THERE

While recounting the moments lived in the pandemic, I ached for that life, the way it used to be; before it all began. It was one which I still crave for, to be returned to me. Every day was not alike, but each day surely used to have a routine that enabled me to be away from a nebulous existence of confinement, we are presently gripped into.

I remember being in bed and beginning my day by snoozing the alarm clock for one time at least, I used to get up even before the sun made its presence; at 5:00 AM, to be precise. After subsequent repetition of my action of delaying my rise, I used to sleepily get ready, brushing my teeth while sleeping all the while! Then I used to head towards my study table to indulge myself in some self-study. It was not that I was very studious, waking up so early just to do so; rather the exciting cum busy schedule of mine prevented me to do so, without any distractions later.

Then I used to arrange my bag, recollecting whether I had packed in all the necessary stuff. It was then I used to remember that I was instructed by one of my teachers to make a poster or any piece of paper exhibiting my creativity on the topic given in the class, the previous day. By then, it used to be late, enough to get some scolding from my mother for showing extra indulgence and further forgetting about it. Helter-skelter, with Google's assistance and my last-minute art skills, I used to try finishing my work on the dining table along with the breakfast, gulping the morsels hurriedly.

Being at a distance away, our school provided enough time for people like me to complete some undone work, although just in time! My parents used to drop me at my bus stop from where I had to take the school bus to my destination. While in our car, the back seat used to be flooded with sketches, colours and other stationery, constantly being used by me to finish off the project. It used to be accompanied by my mother's advice to organise and prioritise things beforehand, to avoid such distress!

When I used to be busy drawing the last stroke, the bus used to blow a loud horn, signaling me to dash into it. And I, bidding bye to my parents, used to charge into it, with the chart paper and colour boxes stuffed in my hands. Seeing my artwork, my bus mates used to welcome me, ready with their questions and unending chatters, even on my way to the seat, left vacant to be occupied by me. Listening to our continuous blabber, the bus conductor used to remark, "You children had met yesterday, and seeing you talk, it seems that it has been quite a while!" And we used to respond to him with a chorus laugh.

As our school bus used to be ready to be parked at the spacious parking lot of our school, we used to get ready with our bags to rush to our respective classes, parting ways with each other until afternoon. Rushing to the class, I used to stop midway talking to my friends who happened to run into me in the corridor. Our conversation could only be disrupted when the first bell rang, heralding us to lead ourselves into the assembly ground. Being the class monitor, I used to lead the line in a systematic way. Our morning assembly comprised of a lot of contents, ranging from prayers and daily news to monotonous announcements to pledge, finally ending with our national anthem. Sometimes it also used to be complemented with enthralling quizzes or exercise sessions conducted by our PT teacher.

After standing still in the scorching sun for nearly half an hour, we used to head back to our classes, to begin with some studies and obviously, lots of fun! Our attendance used to be marked with the initial fun triggered by one of our classmates, who happened to be dozing off while his name was called! Post attendance, our class teacher used to begin the Maths class by asking questions, inciting many to ask, "Ma'am, may I go to the washroom?" or "May I go to fill my water bottle?" And pleas like these used to be put down by targeting these smart students! In a similar fashion, the first two periods used to be spent, with people making an effort to try their lucks to escape!

Then our water break or the mini lunch break used to begin, compelling most of the students to finish their lunch boxes to be free to play and talk during the 45 minute-long break, the anticipated interval. But before it, we used to undergo another three periods, with Science being the important one. Our science teacher was the strictest of all we had ever seen, always making our uncontrollable class silent once and for all. This used to be the time when none of us dared to play our pranks. The 'complaint box' of our class, an artificially driven sincere student used to utilise this period to irritate us by trying to volunteer unnecessarily for all the jobs assigned by the teacher. Luckily we had to tolerate her for that period only, as she used to retreat to her cocoon of silence soon after! Interval, our most awaited time used to swing us into fun as soon as the bell rung, ignoring the teacher who had mistakenly asked us to submit our notebooks!

With other periods, post-interval passing by lazily, sometimes we suddenly used to be confronted by a surprise test. This used to make the whole class panic, rushing back to the textbook that had been boycotted since long! The test used to be completed with the teacher snatching the answer sheets one by one! Finally, in the end, we used to have our Hindi class, which used to be filled with peals of laughter, owing to our simpleton sir, falling prey to the pranks of our mischievous pals. There were times when most of our class used to be out for some important work assigned by another teacher, which was mainly for some excursion in the last period. And our innocent teacher used to believe in students who used to have problems like headache, unconsciousness, stomachache, and what not, almost six times a week! This used to be a routine affair, with people acting smart.

At the end of school, we used to rush to our buses, exhausted by the day's bonhomie! And we were left at our bus stops, from where our guardians took charge of their wards back home.

Reaching home, I used to finish my lunch and later some school work. Subsequently, as the pendulum clock heralded the time 4:00 pm, I used to head towards the equitation area, riding my sturdy bicycle. I did not really get to know the day when I started liking and pursuing horse riding, which once used to be a waterloo and was disliked by me! After an hour of practice, I used to change into my sports wear to go for my badminton coaching. There, my playmates used to be waiting for me to sweat together, following the rigorous but wonderful training session!

This was an account of a working day, that is, a school day. The scenario was a lot different even during holidays with lots of leisure at hand. With this pandemic in sight even days like Sundays had lost their importance, the way they used to be respectfully treated and always craved for. During the pandemic, initial lockdown days in specific made us lose the week-long longing for relaxation on Sundays! The holidays used to begin with getting up late, followed by a wholesome breakfast or brunch, at times. The entire day used to be spent, engaged in studies during the first half of the day and enjoying the second half to the fullest. In the evening, we used to be at the theatres, watching some newly released movie, with our friends sitting by our sides, holding a can of coke and popcorn! Later, we used to go to the club where we used to enjoy the DJ night and weekly tambola sessions! The awesome food, wonderful company of friends, and the fun-filled environment used to make us chill yet another weekend!

It was all great, to live a life in the pre-pandemic days, devoid of the virus and its effects. All days were not equally good, but way better than the ones we had been forcefully pushed into!

Many special days like my birthday, parents' anniversary went by with no charm, except being together, but with a strong resolve to celebrate it even harder once we get ourselves out of this panic. Sooner things will be fine and the normal days will be back. I hope and pray so.

Chapter 20

HOPE AND OPPORTUNITIES: AMIDST THE ADVERSITY

I t has been more than a year now. And it is really hard to believe that an entire year has gone by, adjusting to the new normal. Amid this inscrutable pandemic, we have even got matric results for the anticipated exams that could not be conducted due to the same unbidden calamity. Moreover, it is still hard to believe that we have not heard the end of this corona till this date.

Post the announcement of the cancellation of my board exams, I had some extra time at my behest. Yes! the eagerly awaited 'usual' session ending break. And I tried to fruitfully utilise it. The year, which actually never was a period to remember; as people barely earned their living, many battled hard finding a source of livelihood for themselves and several suffered over the emotions and anxiety for someone close to have been infected or even lost lives. Our routines also changed. Restrictions became the order of the time. And I collated all such anecdotes which echoed my consciousness, full of uncertainties but also of hope amidst despair during the pandemic and kept refuge in my heart for recognition.

As the history unfolds, every disease has a journey. It has a beginning, painful coverage and even a hopeful end. But some diseases become little more than epidemics. And the world history is replete with such stories. The corona virus is also such an epidemic that turned into a pandemic. But how will posterity remember this period? Surely this phase will be dark enough to navigate towards good things and events to remember as, in hindsight, it has given us many positive lessons and vibes to turn into opportunities for the future.

My little bag of lessons contained a multitude of episodic tales of heroes of the crisis, both as caregivers and sufferers for their resilience to fight back, also of human relationships and connections, of the deprived physical touch, of tears and even of astounding laughter. In a nutshell, it taught us resilience, hope and survival against the unprecedented era of darkness.

For students like me, it was like toiling day and night for the board examinations, without going to school and having any physical accessibility to the guidance of the teachers. The way of learning changed a lot. I was surprised to go through statistics that stated that nearly 35 crores of students were barred from their basic fundamental rights of attaining education in the schools because of this COVID-19 pandemic. Such were the levels to which pandemic had disrupted the usual lives of common students like us.

And as the mode of education switched over to a new form, even we had to get accustomed to it. But before this, we realised a sort of inarguable prejudice created by the new pedagogy. Digitised learning discriminated against those who could not access the internet. This way, only the lucky ones could continue learning without any posed obstacle. Apart from this, we were also no longer able to take up all the activities, which we once dearly enjoyed. Moreover, those were actually one of the few aspects, reducing the gap between theory and practice in actual life. The co-curricular activities, SUPW assignments, the projects, the dramatics to represent any social evil or situation, the game field could no longer enthusiastically involve us; hence debarred us from being prepared for the spirit of teamwork and creativity. Above all, the last few months have been super stressful, also because of the rumours, repeated postponements and finally the cancellation of the board examinations, taking an unwarranted toll on us.

And once our exams finally got cancelled, the results were supposed to be based on qualitative and quantitative reports of the students. The school authorities were brainstorming the procedures and even our parents' views were cordially invited. Everyone ideated to come to a consensus on the criteria to decide on our future. We were given some projects as last-minute assignments to be submitted. One of such projects involved our little minds brainstorming regarding the positive things which this COVID gave us and the society. Initially, like others, I too dragged my mind beyond the walls of fear, anxiety, and distress to find something positive. After speaking at length to each other, collectively as classmates, we found many such points to cheer about and feel good because of the COVID.

Although this made almost all of us crave for the 'old normal', there had been some undeniable silver linings too. We were learning our lessons amidst our comfort zones. Though there was no travelling time involved in commuting, we missed the gossiping school bus travel. The world became a global digital village. We could listen to a motivational webinar hosted by one of our KVIIT alumni scientists, staying in the US, arranged by the school for all of us, just by sitting in front of our screens.

And this offered yet another advantage to students who despite wanting to ask a doubt, used to refrain from asking, in order not to show their inability to grasp the concept. Thus unlike getting afraid to ask our doubts time and again in the classes, each one of us could go through the concepts by playing the video multiple times. We realised that we had indeed galloped into the future in terms of technological vistas.

While sitting idle in my room, I remember to have distinctively heard the chirping sounds of the birds and nature flourished to levels which we had only heard our grandparents talking about, because of the pollution level which had come down drastically. Within days of lockdown, the quality of air and water bodies also improved to an extent that could not have been possible in our world which was gripped with the rivalry

of development until recently. Courtesy of the prolonged lockdowns, the flora and fauna got enough time to rejuvenate in our 'previously' unravelling ecosystem. People could notice faint panoramic views of the mountain ranges just from the outskirts of faraway cities. That was how nature was recuperating. From bouncing back of the world's endangered species in the lockdown to a sharp decline in the number of crimes all over the world, probably this period of confinement was not all evil, specifically for our bountiful nature. What the UN had been trying to do for years, the novel virus did in just a matter of few months!

This period also reminded us that 'less is more' when access to essentials was not there. Many of us realised the essence of the very lines, our mothers had been trying to teach us, "Don't waste your food" but not many of us seemed to get the hang of it, failing to understand that many were struggling to get even the bites we used to leave for the garbage bin stack. I for sure promised myself never to waste food or any of such valuable resources and value every bit which came my way.

We also got enough time to start with our hobbies or passions, which otherwise got little or no attention. The pre-pandemic 'not getting much time syndrome' provided us enough of it to start something, we always thought of or our parents kept telling us to start with. To do away with the initial lockdown boredom, I found inspiration in reading and writing something creative. Commensurately, I began writing daily. And believe me; I enjoyed every bit of it. Learning was really fun that way!

We also saw communication with a different view. Yes, with a total embargo on the movement, we were not able to visit friends and relatives. This pandemic, in reality, helped me regain communication; brewing happy times with my family by eating together, planting a sapling collectively, speaking to dear ones apart regularly and also reaching out to dear friends in need, though telephonically. I came to appreciate that the home-cooked food, prepared by my parents, particularly by my father, tasted way better when eaten in front of the home theatre with everyone rather than any of the known, flashy, overcrowded and superficial corners of the malls in the city!

As I come to the end of my episodic tales and experiences now, I understand that time and tide will pass quickly, maybe letting us forget how we went through these difficult ones, but I will certainly treasure the moments lived during these trying times, forever. Once I refer to it, I for sure will remember the opportunities I got apart from the cruel tales and adversities we lived.

Today, I am excited about my higher secondary classes. I will be in senior school. I am blessed that COVID gave me stories to tell to the next generation, filled with emotions, adversities and even opportunities that lie ahead.